MOONLIT

MOONLIT

Stories by
Antonio López-Ortega

translated from the Spanish by
Nathan Budoff

Lumen Editions
a division of Brookline Books

ISBN 1-57129-057-5

Library of Congress Cataloging-In-Publication Data
Lopez Ortega, Antonio, 1957-
    [Lunar. English.]
    Moonlit: stories / by Antonio Lopez Ortega ; translated from the
Spanish by Nathan Budoff.
        p.   cm.
    ISBN 1-57129-057-5
    I. Budoff, Nathan, 1962-   . II. Title.
PQ8850.22.064L8613   1998
863--dc21   98-33715
                                                                                 CIP

Lunar has appeared in the following Spanish-language editions:
    Fondo Editorial Fundarte, Caracas, Venezuela (1997).
    Universidad Metropolitana de México, México City, México (1998).
    Universidad de Antioquia, Medellín, Colombia (1998).

Cover painting by Nathan Budoff.
Cover design, book design and typography by Erica L. Schultz.

Printed in USA by Data Reproductions Corporation, Auburn Hills, MI.

10 9 8 7 6 5 4 3 2 1

Published by
Lumen Editions
a division of Brookline Books
P.O. Box 1047
Cambridge, Massachusetts 02238
Order toll-free: 1-800-666-BOOK

Contents

I. MOONLIT

Running over its weave
this clear clear moon
holds the spider awake

— *José Juan Tablada*

This book was written, to a large degree, thanks to a fellowship from the Rockefeller Foundation, which allowed me to work in their Bellagio Study Center in Italy during August and September of 1994, and I would like to offer them this evidence of my gratitude.

I.

MOONLIT

Nuptials

The newlyweds arrive in Paris from Caracas. They put up in a small hotel in the Rue des Écoles. He opens the bedroom window the following morning to breathe—he says—the autumnal air of the city of light, while she tremulously rolls over under the sheets. For breakfast they have croissants which they dip slowly in two open-mouthed cups of café au lait.

They weave and interweave an endless conversation which they sprinkle with amorous gestures. He takes in the pallid cheekbones of that extraordinary face and she lets herself be hugged by arms that give her goosebumps. They see something like happiness in the watery mirror of a fountain in the Luxembourg Gardens and they imagine Marie Antoinette strolling along the promenades of Versailles Castle. Subtle are the gestures of holding hands over the Seine and complex the nocturnal maneuvers with which he creates and destroys figures of flesh over her insatiable body.

At the end of the third night, commenting upon a late Debussy opera, they fall into in a café in the Rue d'Auber. The couple at a neighboring table intercedes in the conversation and prolongs the evening. During four hours adorned with glasses of wine, they jump from Rodin to lunar craters and from the nocturnal silhouette of Avila to the immutability of Pont des Arts.

He tests out *le trou normand* when the friendly couple offers to give them a ride to their hotel. Three blocks before they arrive, the French woman asks for cigarettes. They stop the car before a tabac and, diligent, he gets out to buy a pack.

A thousand times he has told and retold the incident: he returns to the car and it's no longer there. A violent start-up, a screaming of tires, the car that disappears forever down a barely lit avenue.

He remembers returning to the hotel and screaming incoherently at the night manager. He ends up at the police station where he shows passports and they make him reconstruct in detail the sequence of the night's events.

After a week of investigation they have him approve a spoken portrait of his wife which the police guarantee they will send to all the border posts and to the consular delegations.

Back in Caracas, a year later, a dry letter from the French embassy mentions the phrase "white slave traffic." Interpol assures him they have a clue in Syria and a consul in Algeria admits to similar episodes of a certain trade in western women.

In the twilight of his bedroom, when he is unable to come to terms with sleep, the man nourishes the unchanging memory of his bride and rails against the false destiny of that insatiable body.

Capillary

La Lupe pulled out her hair. She pulled it out. A bare and unconscious hand—her own hand—slid down over the sleepy sheets and came to rest on her delicate little head from which it abruptly extracted a tuft.

We saw her when she was three—she was a runny-nosed kid—with her crown of sheared hair: a ford of short grass over which no river ran.

Her young mother tried to lighten the load of her crown by shearing her hair in a crew cut. Now it seemed more like the brush of a Roman centurion as she hid herself carelessly among the branches of the only flowering flamboyan tree in the garden.

While the moon shone, the home changed: Grandfather fell to his knees struck down by a heart attack, Grandmother practiced yoga—a white elephant in convulsions—and Mother changed jobs every three months.

The mother's boyfriends—a cunning architect, an aviator with exaggerated eyes, a thick-handed veterinarian—watched Lupe grow: the little crown broadened until it was covered with a disorderly mane that brushed her eighteen-year-old waist.

Strange exercises—a summer camp in Boconó, the steep and rocky trail that let her see the ocean from the peak of Naiguatá, wild beaches which she reached with friends, accessible only in jeeps—gradually distanced her from the vague home and her mother.

A twilight call—in that moment the mother removes the veterinarian's big hands from her left breast—finds Lupe hanging by her feet from the Los Chorros viaduct. The elastic of a bungee cord had allowed her to hug the vacuum of a fall and swing innumerable times—the hair rose and fell like a tide—in a total sacrifice.

In the background of that valley that her entranced eyes recorded among the infinite hair, beyond the city of Caracas, one persistent image: that of her mother raped at sixteen years of age and her unknown father.

Identity

Unare seemed like a safe destination to Manuel. It's Friday and his watch displays twelve noon. He impatiently counts the minutes as the three final students turn in their seats, taking his exam. He already sees himself near Barlovento, chewing up the highway, on the curves, and losing his gaze among the *riquirriquis* that sprout in a disorderly fashion from the ditches along the shoulder.

Passing Caucagua he feels that his chest is wide: the air is a viscous substance that tears at his lungs. Arriving at El Guapo he pushes a cassette his son has left into the player, and an ancient chant of Greek origin springs forth; for a few moments it makes his hair stand on end. He doesn't know why the chanting seems so mournful, as though a woman— the singer—were crying over the loss of a loved one.

He opens the van's four windows. A steamy breeze sticks to his back and permeates his shirt. The crowns of thick trees begin to block the sky while the singer lowers her voice to a sharp thread.

It seems useless to maneuver before what crosses in front of him. He just barely has time to reconstruct the sequence:

a bird of prey has rapidly crossed the highway and landed awkwardly in the back seat. The animal flaps its wings ferociously and Manuel tries to pull over onto the shoulder.

Now they are face to face: Manuel confronts the robust gaze of the hawk and admires its royal scowl. Without thinking, as if by reflex, he stretches out his hand. The animal responds by squeezing its talons into his arm and leaving his sleeve in tatters. A light clawing has cut open a line of blood on his arm.

The animal jumps up and down on the seat. It measures the opening of the window through which it squeezed itself and finally manages to lift into flight after thunderously smashing its wings against the frame of the car door.

Manuel sits startled and alone with the Greek singer. The murmuring voice can almost be mistaken for silence. Suddenly he pushes the flip button and he encounters the repetitive melody of Albinoni's "Adagio."

He doesn't know why he runs his finger over and over the thread of blood and then sucks on it.

— *for Manuel Espinoza*
(to whom the story belongs)

Bellagio

My father cultivated a painting. He bought it in Bachaquero—a vendor passed by the country houses once a week—and he hung it on the dining room's widest wall. The painting presided over all our meals, all the screaming of childhood, an occasional misplaced slap during some reprimand. I have wanted to reconstruct the image of the painting: an old and decrepit house is bathed by the faint waves of a lake that separates the paint from its stairway. It's a yellowish house, tall and suspended in the air, with a side staircase that rises from the surface of the lake. I always knew that the stairs continued underwater and I imagined them slippery, covered with moss and snails.

Sometime later I found out that the picture—primitive, nostalgic, realist—reproduces an image from Como Lake in Italy. They have spoken to me of mountains that plunge abruptly into the lake, of villages forced to perch on the last border of sand that the earth grudgingly offers.

They have also spoken to me of a headland in the form of a peninsula from where you can see the whole lake, settled originally by the Ligurians, a peaceful people who watched from antiquity the transit of Etruscans, Celts, Teutons, Greeks and Venetians.

I have always known that this painting from my childhood foreshadowed my death. And now that, at the end of my days, I stroll slowly towards the peak of the headland, where a refined woman had the Villa Serbelloni reconstructed, I feel that the cycle is closing, that every beginning contains its own dénouement.

The Human Voice

Professor James Ljunggren, a British subject of Swedish descent, has lectured at the University of Reading since he was a young man. His book *The Regulation of Oxygen by Photosynthetic Carbon Metabolism* placed him at the summit of biochemical studies. Students from Latin America and Australia have followed him for years and they have jostled one another to obtain a seat in such illuminating lectures.

They recount that an automobile accident in the suburbs of Hamburg condemned him to a life of locomotive paralysis. It took months for Ljunggren to rehabilitate himself, and one spring afternoon he reappeared in a self-propelled wheelchair that climbed up any hill and introduced him into all the corridors that opened before his eyes. His gaze, noted his followers, was no longer the sharp arrow of his younger days but a litany that lost itself in the landscape.

Submerged in her husband's tragedy, Janice was diligent and loving from the start. She changed bandages in the hospital, she lifted weights together with him, she cleared the obstacles from public paths and searched for alternative destinies to university life.

Year after year August gradually imposed its rhythm, and not a summer passed when they didn't visit a little hotel on the shore of Como Lake where the moon shined like an insomniac eye.

One night's urge led them to attend an original operetta by Jean Cocteau in a reconstructed country home. *La voce umana* was interpreted by a blond soprano who modulated a strange version of Poulenc translated into Italian.

They say that in the sharpest moments, when the ancient walls absorbed the screams of the soprano, Janice caressed the bar of the wheelchair as if she were squeezing James' hand.

Fried Eggs

Carlucho dabs his bread in the fried egg. He's been dipping it since he was three years old and now he's sixteen. On vacation in Adícora, camping in Borubata, or eating breakfast in a kiosk by the river in Choroní, he orders fried eggs.

We celebrate his exploit quietly, without any great commentaries. Aunt Luisa—his mother—kept three hens in the yard of the old house in Quinta Crespo where they lived, and the whole family—she said—had to eat the chicken's eggs. There were a lot of eggs, really, for so few family members: Uncle Delio maneuvering tankers in the Adriatic, in the North Sea, in the gray bay of Rotterdam; his sister Ana always eating lunch in her classmates' houses—she studied architecture and the poor girl was always pulling all-nighters; and the oldest, Pablo, had been in a boarding school in Santa Cruz de Tenerife for years.

Well, all the eggs ended up crossing Carlucho's palate— a slow, calm, ruminating palate, we should add. "There's no yolk like the home-grown one," Aunt Luisa would say. "Without hormones: bright orange."

In the restaurants, while he went to the men's room to

wash his hands, we would order for Carlucho: chicken sandwiches, bacon cheeseburgers, pizzas with double cheese ... and our cousin always returned to his fried eggs.

We wanted—even now we are still trying—to define with precision the origin of that fixation. We think we have found it (though it's only a hypothesis that we frequently interchange with other possibilities) in the sudden death of Aunt Luisa, run over by a truck in El Paraíso as she returned from shopping.

At the wake we only saw her chest and face—somewhat swollen. Her legs, it seems, were completely destroyed.

Carlucho continues day after day encrusting the crumbs of his bread into that concentric yellow circle. The news of his mother's death reached him when he was only six years old, while he ate breakfast. It's true that it took Uncle Delio a full month to reach La Guaira: he cried for Aunt Luisa in his cabin on the high sea. We all missed him at the funeral.

Clay Figurines

There's nothing like the sound of rain, heard from bed. A strange emotion grows inside you as catastrophes unfold outside. I have cultivated this exercise since childhood, with an infinite apprehension. Well, you'll understand that my preference falls back on the hot sweaty nights when not even a hint of wind is blowing. You go to bed with the assurance that deep in the night, rolling over suffocated in the sheets, you'll awake in the middle of a vigorous downpour, one of those that feel like the sky is tumbling down. Everything begins with a flapping of doors and windows, with languid curtains suddenly confused, with a coolness that enters the bedroom swiftly like a living creature. You awaken in the middle of the vitality that things have suddenly taken on, and your initial response is fear. You tend to wrap yourself up, cover yourself in the blankets, without realizing that you have been sweating profusely deep into the night and that a damp ring traces the circumference of your neck. Then you get up and walk around, you don't know why but you walk, you lean out the window, you watch the spastic dance of the sandbox tree's branches from its roots right up to its crown,

thirsty for water, and you cheer up. Afterwards it will be all
ears, ears for the rain: the thunder, the fallen branches of the
trees, the house surprisingly animated by the doors that slam,
the humming that wedges in the corridors, objects that fall,
the air acquiring a real, tangible, authoritarian body, which
nothing dares oppose. The next step will be a wait, the long
wait of a listener who cannot fall asleep, who rolls over and
over in bed without respite, who seems to want to guard that
wet distance from this useless cloister which offers nothing
to the general dynamics of water.

Rain is our winter: an instant of momentary evaluation
in which we grow in solitude among objects. It's difficult to
find a more intimate moment than that of inhabiting the
rain. I prove it yet again as I aimlessly night-walk around the
house, yearning to participate in the clamor that governs all
the space around me. And it's as if an impulse which I can't
quite decipher wants to venture outside and head off some
sense of belonging to all that is happening around me. Then,
like an exercise in futility, I try to distance myself from the
blind mechanics with which my mind is threading together
the images of past rainstorms, inexorably to bring back a
sticky afternoon in Lagunillas where I find myself still in the
company of Hernán and Daniel.

We were playing in a park in Las Delicias on a recently
planted lawn which formed irregular mounds, when we perceived a black cloud that darkened the day in seconds. There
was construction at one end of the park, and we concentrated on an especially long slide (one had to count thirty
aluminum steps in the ladder that led to the apex). The slide
down was fast and we went down with our feet high in the

air to cushion the final impact of our curled-up bodies.

We began to receive the drops striking like pebbles and we suddenly created a new game which consisted of sliding down each time with greater velocity, as the slide was now more glossy and slippery. A complicit sleepless happiness pulls us on, and disobeying our mothers—surely our snacks are ready by now—we go on soaking ourselves like dishcloths. Our hair dripping; our faces brilliant with sweat; our shoes permeated like sponges; our pants heavy.

· Hernán—with his thick lenses all fogged up—suddenly says good-bye and leaves us, heading towards his house. He goes running off through the back part of the park and he takes a short cut crossing through the construction site. We watch him go off into the gaseous film of the rain with his mustard-color flannel shirt and, without understanding, we see the earth suck him in up to his chest. Hernán lets out two or three screams and Daniel and I run, jumping over the puddles that form in the grass. We discover him submerged up to his waist in the middle of a pool of clay that, evidently, had formed in one of the ditches excavated by the workers, and we see how he struggles uselessly to get out of the quicksand.

The rain becomes stronger—little bullets strike our naked arms—and visibility becomes difficult. Hernán becomes frightened upon making no progress and he starts to cry dry tears. His hands slowly splash the surface and his torso sinks a little bit with every movement. Daniel, who has slipped in the mud as he approached one of the borders of the pool, retreats stumbling and looks at me as though he were searching for an answer. I look around in all directions: there are

bricks, bags of cement, pieces of wood, buckets, picks, shovels and a cement mixing machine with its mouth staring at
the sky. Nothing specific occurs to me: should I throw solid
objects into the mud (wood or bricks) to offer more support,
should I stretch my arm out to Hernán (Daniel and I form a
chain in a useless gesture), should I run to one of our family's
houses in search of help...

Suddenly, old and frayed, I see it. It's a rope that en-
circles the plastic tarp over the bags of cement. I gesture to
Daniel opening my eyes as wide as possible. We go over to
the tarp and try to untie it. It's hopeless. I opt instead for one
of the shovels and, aiming the sharp metal edge at one of the
knots, I hit it desperately. We never knew how we managed
to do it: undoubtedly, the shovel was heavy for our young
bodies. I hit it and I hit it again and I note that the rope is
yielding in an apathetic tangle of strands. The cord detaches
itself from its binds and I grab one end—Daniel takes the
other—to encircle the pool of clay. We slowly bring the rope
in from both extremes and we are able to slide it level with
the surface until we bump into Hernán's body. Now the cord
crosses his chest and it folds backwards beneath his under-
arms, creating a sort of lever that allows us to tense it up and
pull Hernán towards one of the banks. Daniel and I, red-
dened from the effort, saw the mustard flannel completely
covered with mud and the glasses covered with water vapor
floating insensibly before his near-sighted eyes. Daniel, stretch-
ing himself, was the first to give him a hand. We finished
pulling him out like a heavy sack of potatoes in a mess of
hands and feet that included all three of us. We stay there,
on the edge, for seconds—the drops were hitting us—with-

out understanding anything, looking into each other's faces and containing the happiness of knowing we were all together. Later we made a pact, an inviolable pledge in the rain, not to speak a single word of what had happened to our mothers. We would invent some pretext to justify the dominant brown tone of our clothes.

I feel that sudden rainstorm and that spontaneous mud puddle persecute me. I'll never be safe from that scene. I awake at night, under any storm, and it's as if I want to stretch my arm out to Hernán, I still see him splashing with anguish in the pool of my days.

The Tree of Forgetfulness

Alfonso and Siri—he Chilean, she Norwegian—met as youths in Bloomington, Indiana. A concert at the local university— he impressed them with Granados's *Goyescas* and she made a woman in the front row cry with the aria *Mio cor* by Handel— tied them together: she recognized Alfonso's manly integrity and he was seized by Siri's lively gaze.

Since then they have been inseparable. Three grown children, two tenured positions in Bloomington, and a sound-proof studio in the house where they shut themselves up every afternoon constitute the major footprints of their long trek.

Santiago, Valparaíso, Lillehammer, Caracas, Cartagena and Milan are a few of the cities from which they retain images. They enumerate them gradually and with delight and will recount to anyone forty years' events in the half hour they daily dedicate to tea.

We never discovered the source of such harmony. Alfonso

—earthy—can be reserved, observant, distant: Siri—talk-ative—is more social, resonant, cutting. Seeing them together is like observing a gadget, a composition of forces, an inte-gration.

Alfonso unfolds himself in a measured English with His-panic resonances, with a precise and differentiated vocabu-lary. Siri spreads out with a more British accent, with thick, Nordic guffaws, capable of chasing the cold away.

We saw each other in Bellagio, on a typical afternoon, and we understood immediately. Their language was differ-ent: radical, deep, secret. A piece by Ginastera—he on the piano, she the mezzo-soprano—allowed us to discover the source, it returned them to us whole, in the ciphered code that only they shared.

— *for the Montecino duo*

The Face

Many years we've been without news of Olguita Maria, the oldest of the cousins. Icod of the Wine returns her to us now and then—there's a photo of her at the foot of a hundred-year-old Dragon tree—and a few of her mother's, Aunt Olga's, letters.

We wanted forever to imagine her as she was: rebellious, bombastic, aloof. We knew about her eloping with her boyfriend, her communes, her organic diet. She was excommunicated: the family embellished the legend with drugs, debauchery, an illegitimate child.

To the joy of Aunt Olga, with her hair graying, time now returns her to us as a famous professor of Philosophy at the University of Las Palmas, married to the boyfriend she eloped with and with two beautiful children: Alfonso—the one from the commune—and Sonia.

I return to the photo from long ago—I'm hugging her under the tree—and I compare it with the latest one that Aunt Olga has sent. Her face hasn't changed: her eyebrows are still thick, her nose is still thin, her face still retains the deep beauty that disturbed us all.

Branch of a Flowering Lemon Tree

Alberto is in the habit of getting up on Sundays and responding to strange impulses: venturing off on any highway in search of the unknown. One Sunday it could be the hills of San Juan; another, the town of Osma on the central shore; yet another, San Francisco de Yare.

Maruja and the three kids run from him. They know the routine by now: hours and hours of heat; in the best of cases, the cavernous geology of a hill. Sometimes, even, Alberto doesn't bother to get out of the car; he stays sitting in the car as though it were a window on the world, as though within it resided his true home and everything else was strictly foreign.

This time he gets up and asks Maruja to accompany him to the Littoral Central. He doesn't have a specific goal: he talks about going down to Puerto Cruz from Colonia Tovar, going as far as Naiguatá, touring La Sabana. Maruja immediately invents a trip to some museum, kisses him, and abandons him. As far as the kids, don't even mention it: the older one is still asleep (like every Sunday), the middle one is studying for an exam, and the youngest is getting ready to go to his baseball game.

Alberto eats breakfast alone—honey on his pancakes, a generous amount of cream in his coffee—and heads off without a fixed destination. He travels the Autopista del Este like a sleepwalker, he throws himself into the Boquerón tunnel and the blackness seems infinite, he confronts La Guaira and it all seems fetid.

In the port he stops in front of the Casa Guipuzcoana. Lowering his head, he tries to appreciate the Spanish Colonial architecture through the passenger's window. It's useless; he can't appreciate anything. He gives up. He turns the car around in a nearby square and confronts a mural by Cruz Diez. The disagreeable odor of La Guaira confronts him again and his eyes begin to drift off towards the buildings of Maiquetía.

He doesn't know why he detours just before the highway begins and goes down the ramp leaving the airport behind. He's getting closer to Catia La Mar. He sees the electric plant at Tacoa, the Naval Academy at Mamo.

Nothing impresses him very much. Nevertheless, he continues. He tries to remember something, some ride with his father when he was a kid. He's not sure. Suddenly he remembers a name. Tarmas, yes, the town of Tarmas. He doesn't know how to get there but he knows it can't be far away. He asks a traffic officer in Catia La Mar; the policeman doesn't exactly know either. "Keep going up," he tells him, "... it's higher up." He stops at a crossroads: there's a store, kids running around, a parrot tied to a lamppost. He gets out and asks the store owner. "Ten kilometers straight ahead and then you continue climbing to the left," the easygoing black man answers.

He begins to go uphill. The landscape changes. It stops being coastal and converts to mountainous. The ocean spray has disappeared to make way for veils of fog that cross the highway. Everything turns leafy. He begins remembering the ride with his father, reconstructing it, but he's missing details. He's merely playing with fragments: he sees his little knees in the back seat, he's holding a green toy plane made of steel.

The landscape enfolds him. The route is becoming long and steep. Trees with high crowns block the sky; shafts of light cut across the path like spotlights. He sees birds vibrating in the air when the van bucks. He accelerates and the motor doesn't respond. He approaches the edge, taking advantage of the last impulse. He turns the car off and remains seated. It's difficult for him to decide to get out. He thinks that he hasn't seen anyone on the road. Finally, he gets out. Now standing, a burst of cool air receives him.

He likes the substance that envelops his nose: it's an odor that's difficult to describe, the mixture of pure air with fruit. He lifts the hood. He sees the orifice of the hose: a very light stream of vapor escapes the cooling system. He begins to debate what he should do. He stays there, detained, in front of the car, detailing the place: thick vines, guacharacas, a strange humming, a colossal ceiba tree, dizzy. In the distance, neatly, bunches of orchids sprout from the trunk of a samán tree. He lowers his eyes. He sees that the highway is made out of plates of cement: weeds grow in the cracks. He hears the whine of the hose, fading away. He wonders if he should go up or down, if he should try to reach Tarmas or return to the intersection. He has no idea of the distance, of how far he's come, of what still remains to be covered.

He opens the trunk: just a cross wrench, the spare tire. He searches for a rag, some piece of cloth to knot around the hose. It's useless. He closes the trunk. Again he remains standing, absorbed. A guacharaca, precisely, fills the space. He tunes his ear and lets a murmur carry him away: something like music, something like a muffled drum.

He begins walking uphill, counting the cracks between the plates as he goes. Turning and looking back he sees the vehicle: it seems like a ridiculous little object against the mountain. The hike feels good to him; he doesn't rush his pace. He rolls up his sleeves and puts his hands in his pockets. The landscape becomes endless: more tall trees, more lianas, enormous leaves that almost cross the road. For a second, he wants to go back, begin the descent to the car, further down, even. Opt for something known: a filling station in Catia La Mar, a mechanic working the Sunday shift. But he lets himself get carried along, he lets inertia carry him along. The murmur gradually grows clearer: music wrapped in a whole uproar. And then, on an abrupt curve in the road, another ceiba tree: thick, majestic, unequivocal. He feels shrunken, insignificant. The curve opens onto another valley that illustrates how long the road stretches out before him; the highway goes snaking around the foothills of successive mountains. In the distance, higher up, where the highway seems to disappear, he sees something whitish, maybe a house.

He stops again. His sleeves are wet, his chest palpitating. He sees a clear trail along the side of the highway. He walks over to it and sees how it goes downhill in a shortcut and then climbs again to the whitish spot in the distance. He doesn't know what to do. He vacillates, looking at the trail, at the sky, at the road. He distinguishes a thread of flattened earth on the trail, and enters with fear, looking in all directions. There are footprints: big, small, a few filled with water. Going down, the trail seems safe, navigable. He extends his arms and goes along separating branches.

The trail gradually widens and opens up. He comes to a little clearing where the vegetation is lower and hears a murmur: water flowing between rocks, a river. The trail becomes flooded: his shoes get wet, they splash bits of mud that land on his pants. He sees three big, solid rocks in the course of the river. He stops a moment: it's a noble stream of water, sprinkled with vegetation. He jumps onto the first rock, he jumps onto the second. He tries to land on the third and his foot slips on a film of moss. He falls on his back, in the middle of the course of the creek. His head ends up hitting the second rock; his feet have remained caught on the third. Water bathes his whole trunk. It's a cool, agreeable current. His gaze goes cloudy, everything vibrates, double images appear. He closes his eyes and tries opening them again, the images are still double. Pain paralyzes him; his head throbs, a stabbing pain grows in his back. Still he lies there. He tries to sit up and his body doesn't respond. He looks at the sky—double, the branches—double, the spiny trunk of a sandbox tree—double. The water soothes the pain in his back, it drugs it. He opens and closes his eyes, indefinitely, and thinks of his father, of the long-ago journey. He still lacks the power to reunite the fragments: his knees, his green airplane, his face barely leaning out the window.

Another bright guacharaca, and the distant noise that is becoming musical. He begins to get scared, a dry scream escapes him. The water runs over and under his body, he can feel it precisely. A button on his shirt rises and falls with the flow of the water. He feels a fatigue, a desire to abandon himself, to sleep. He sees Maruja in the museum, he tries to imagine her, he sees their children. He sees his father again, clouded. He resists falling asleep, he knows he shouldn't let himself get dragged down by drowsiness. He tries, just a bit, to lower his head. The movement causes a sharp, central pain. He manages to bring his face level with the surface of the water, a bubbling current passes between his eyes, it wakes him up.

He sees himself from above. It's a strange sensation but he sees himself from above, thrown down, abandoned. He sees double, his body in double, encrusted in the flow of the river. He wakes up, he wakes up from what he believes he has dreamed. He feels the uproar drawing closer, now he can distinguish voices, drums, melodies. He cheers up and tries to raise his arms. The arms respond, yes. He sees his palm, double, before his eyes; he sees his two palms. He wants to concentrate, to avoid the drifting off which is so inviting. He discovers a key and tries to concentrate on the noise, he knows that the music, barely distinguishable, will order a sequence for him, will reconstruct a thought.

He gets happier knowing that the music is approaching. He tries to imagine the scene, tries to invent an origin for the drums, for the singing, for the sticks that hit trunks. Suddenly he discovers it; a spurt of water falls in his eyes and he discovers it. It's a procession, of course, and it must be coming down the highway. He raises his hands—his double palm—in an effort to confirm that he's alive, in improvising some sign. He thinks of his father, more fragments come back to him: the country house in Tarmas, the air of Tarmas, the festival of San Juan, the child saint progressing through the multitude.

The pain turns serious, a church bell slowly ringing, a bite that almost reaches his chest. He searches for the music with his ears, he retains it. He lets the pounding of the drums confuse itself with the stabbing, central, radical pain. A drunkenness begins to blanket him. Everything fuses and becomes confused: successive images of Maruja, the children, his father, the green toy plane, the central square of Tarmas, the procession, the holy infant, Maruja again, his father again ... he follows the melody, it sweetens his ears. All the sounds suspend themselves—the guacharacas, the omnipresent murmur of the river, the creaking branches—beneath the melody. He supposes it's a procession, he believes it and he doesn't care if it's true or not. He's falling asleep in the middle of the melody, he's giving himself up, surrendering all his efforts. He deciphers the drums, the clattering of the drums, the female voices. He wants to capture a phrase, yes, a phrase that now he distinguishes, the clear voice of a woman singing, "*Silly, Malembe, a branch of flowering lemon,*" as he abandons himself.

— *for Isabel Loero and the Vasallos*

Footprints

Bernardo lifts a plastic bucket up towards the sky and offers it to me. It's difficult to ignore everything that this gesture represents: to stroll along the shore of the ocean searching for shells, little rocks, fossils, mother of pearl conches, bits of glass smoothed and formed by the ocean, and, if one is lucky, even peonies.

It's a specific exercise, he is five years old as he comes over to me, measures his head against what is almost my belly button, puts his feet up on top of mine to confirm our difference in scale and endeavors to get me to take my first few steps carrying him, playing robot.

We head off on the last hike in Varadero, a tongue of land that extends to the west of Morrocoy. We see the turquoise blue of the ocean hurling itself in frothy waves that are slow to disappear. We wanted to distance ourselves from the other sunbathers—tents, coolers, umbrellas, beach chairs —towards the eastern slope of the beach in a crossing that was ours and ours alone.

This is how the hike began: Bernardito mounted on my feet, the blue bucket hanging from my forearm, the glare obscuring our view and the pace more or less slow, unhurried.

We reach the end of the central bay (now Bernardo is walking on his own and he turns to see his footprints erased by the sea) and we perceive another beach on the right, a wilder one, which opened a passage among craggy rocks, mangroves, fallen tree trunks, stony sand and, at the end, a flat arm of land that abruptly bisected the path and in which I thought I saw caves.

I said that the bay was perfect for the excursion. There we'd encounter a living museum that Bernardo would summarize in his beach bucket, bringing to his mother what for him was still almost a treasure.

Bernardo's fluorescent green bathing suit vibrated over the sand (it seemed to dance by itself against the landscape). His gait was cautious, apprehensive; he had stopped counting his footprints (he didn't stop being proud of that writing that the ocean erased no matter how many times he reinscribed the line of his passage) for this new game in which, jumping from one side to the other, absorbed and amazed, he collected precious stones.

The selection began with great discretion (the smooth spiral of a snail's shell and the ancient trail of a worm over a crimson conch were his favorites) and gradually increased in chaos (a weather-beaten domino topped the mound). I ended up with the bucket in my hands, now that it had gotten rather heavy.

We entered a vast area of sand, almost a small inlet, that opened to our right and contained several tide pools. Bernardo splashed as much as he could and clouded the reflection of his face with the swirling of a stick that he spun in the puddles. The sand was like oatmeal and our feet sank in up to our ankles. The walk turned heavy and clumsy.

We left behind the little cove to confront branches of mangroves extending over the beach. It was the mouth of a channel, no doubt, and I had to carry Bernardo with the water up to my waist to reach the other side. In the middle of the canal, animated by a faint current, I was able to see my feet agitating the sand at the bottom and a little fish that shone like a coin. I had to grab onto the low branch of a mangrove to keep from losing my balance and I noticed that I brought my hand back with a cut: a limy pincer adhering to the branch opened a line of blood on the palm of my hand. I reached the other bank after wetting my hand and letting the red hue dissolve in the transparency of the water. I hid the wound from Bernardo and deposited him again on the sand.

The new stretch welcomed us with a rocky terrain, full of unexpected sharp edges. Bernardo complained and, in a moment, I was at the point of turning back. The peninsula of land now looked close and I got him enthused with the idea of finding a cave. I lifted him up on my shoulders and let my left hand (the other throbbed with the wound) take care of the beach bucket.

I walked slowly, opening my legs until I encountered solid ground. The higher edge of the beach offered bigger rocks, smoothed out, but on the first contact with my foot the needle of heat obliged me to return to the wet stones of the lower reaches. I began to get tired, and to realize that at this point continuing on and returning would be the same thing. I stopped on a black rock (a white line split it into two exact halves) and I sat down with Bernardo on my lap. He was different; he spoke very little and the heat on his shoulders had worn him out. He looked at the ground without fixing his gaze on anything, and he blindly poked with the head of a stick that he arched among the stones.

The spit of land must be about thirty yards away. It was a strange structure amidst the marine environment. On top, the descending flank brought dried-out trees, thistles, loose roots; the point that entered the ocean became a black rock, naked, that parted the tide in two. Only the first part was accessible: the surface seemed porous and through the air holes gushed spurts of water. I animated Bernardo for the last time (the offer of finding a cave was now unavoidable) and I set him once again on my shoulders.

This last stretch didn't vary: the strip of beach narrowed between a high bank of sand and the rocky trail we were coming from. My feet continued arched, testing every stretch of the surface. Time felt suspended: only the water moved in brusque, surprising fluctuations.

We had the wall before us, a wall that parted the path at its roots. Crabs crawled over it from top to bottom, weaving a nervous script, and the pores expelled spurts of high-pressured water. Suddenly, I understood: the spit retained the ocean and surely held back strong surges of waves from the other side which sent minor emissaries through the openings on this side as best they could. The spurts varied from lines of water that snaked over the surface to forceful instantaneous showers that turned into spray. Bernardo let himself be overtaken by this misty bath that inundated him, and he began to scramble along the foot of the wall like a revived creature. It was evident that there were no caves: just barely initial orifices which the ocean had not yet burrowed with sufficient force.

I wanted to let myself be carried along by the moment, by the coolness that bathed my chest and overheated feet. I sat down on a crag along the side and looked at all of the return trail that awaited us. My hand pulsed slowly; the water had closed the wound, drawing a reddish, meaty line. Bernardo pulled out the relics from his bucket and let the spray that washed over them give them new forms.

The Refrigerator

Maybe the story demands only one phrase, a four-line sequence. It's Liana who swells it up and turns it incisive (or maybe it's Alvaro's final comment). We have lost track, of course, of Liana. The last we heard wasn't pleasant: her father—an opulent rancher from Apure—sent her to Cambridge to study English, and in a pub in Market Square she met an Indian man who practically lowered her to the category of servant (the girl from Caracas let herself be subjugated by this living demon, and they say that in the final stage of her hell she was even willing to sell heroin). But this isn't the chapter we wish to recreate; it would be better, we should say, to eliminate it, erase it from a register which returns her to us exuberant, adolescent, ingenuous.

With Liana, it must be said, we traveled the whole country: we ate barnacles in Mantecal, Andean *arepas* in Aparteaderos, fresh grouper in Píritu. It was an excessive, opulent exercise, that went so far as to include chauffeurs, private planes and rental cars.

It was the currency she offered in exchange for a never-defined friendship, always dependent on mechanisms which she kept hidden. Without being aware of it, Liana actually offered herself in every gesture of courtesy, as if there was nothing worldly, as if everything were a pact negotiated under the table. Liana divested herself of we don't know what, Liana overflowed.

We took her in, we gave her membership in the club. And we made her laugh, sure, we made her laugh until she cried with a mocking humor that she couldn't escape (we should say, more accurately, that she herself brought on). So, climbing in with the chauffeur, traveling in her father's private plane, or attending her fifteenth birthday party with valets and carriages included, was the appropriate terrain for immediate parody, for mockery. And Liana acceded to it, she amiably acceded.

We want to reconstruct one lonely episode: A trip to Playa Colorada, where her family had a beach house. The preparations were infinite, with a disproportionate anticipation. Her mother, Rocío the Spanish servant, the chauffeur ... all were participants in the conspiracy, that is: the excursion.

After having postponed the trip for three consecutive weekends (the mockery began, it began: Carlos, for example, said that the house didn't exist; Gustavo, that the advertised mansion was nothing more than a reformed fisherman's cabin), we finally left in three cars, a group of twelve.

We arrived at the house (a normal abode, furnished with the typical equipment of a beach house) and we installed hammocks, coolers full of ice, radios in the bedrooms, fans in the corners, portable tables in the living room for the nightly game of cards, fresh sheets on the beds for the girls, food in the pantry, bottles of rum in the cabinet and food in the refrigerator. The refrigerator ... Alvaro was the first to open it and burst out retching. He hurled the door closed and crossed the living room doubled over heading for the bathroom at the back. The refrigerator ... well, it was foul, unapproachable. "Don't open it, shit, don't open it," he screamed, gripping the bowl. Some power outage, we later deduced, had deactivated it, and a dozen rotten eggs (we were reminded of *Alien*, the movie) decayed the environment. Our enthusiasm went through the floor. A few, the most affected, fled immediately to the beach (they confirmed that they improvised a hut with palm leaves in the sand); others, the less affected, remained in the house to make a show of our presence and not leave Liana alone (nobody, of course, would confront the cleaning of the refrigerator).

We then see Liana calling Caracas (and this is a scene that we can't erase, that repeats itself and repeats itself: her expression of desolation, her helplessness, her way of asking for things). She speaks to Rocío, to her mother, to her father. She hangs up the telephone. Now her father has made arrangements: Rocío will come immediately in an express taxi to clean the refrigerator (a journey of three hours, which we could easily spend on the beach, amid palm trees and rum).

Rocío arrived (nobody saw her; all of us imagined her). She confronted the refrigerator almost like the pass of a bull before a bullfighter. She opened it in one daring move (her strength, her determination had to overwhelm the eggs, turn them insignificant). She wore a bandanna over her mouth. She threw her body and all of herself into that Gothic cav-

ern, into that sewer of putrid waters, and came out victori-
ous, supreme, shining. She climbed back into the taxi and
returned to the great city.

Afterwards we added up the costs: a special salary for
Rocío because it was her day off, the charge for an express
taxi on a holiday, the cleaning supplies and disinfectants ...
it all added up to a small fortune.

We returned from the beach to make peace with the
cleanliness. And then the detail, the detail that remains,
that still enlivens us: Alvaro's prompt comment while we
were playing that night's sixth hand of poker amid rum and
beers: "Pay me that much and I swear I'll lick the refrigerator
clean with my tongue."

Sand Castle

For starters: a Sunday excursion, the fallen leaves, police horses, a clear meadow with cows at the end of the hike. Lucía's ritual: run around with caution, corn for the pigeons, cotton candy, the slide in the playground, the images of Juan Andrés, little feet kicking up leaves, little hands in coat pockets (in winter), rosy cheeks, sweets for variety and, at the end, immovable, a beach bucket to make the sand castle.

Don't even mention the zoo. Entering there would carry us to another plane. We leave aside the playful seals, the indifferent lion, the slow boa that nobody could shock and the chimpanzee that always showed his teeth to Magdalena.

Well, we return to the essential: our successive Sundays in the Bois de Vincennes, its precise timing: a bus from Place de la Nation, food and drinks in the backpack, sometimes a camera. Rubber-soled shoes, short excursions for the children and the playground where, I repeat, we always open out into the land of Juan Andrés' plastic bucket.

But this time we wanted to lose ourselves in, how should I say it, a frank state of desperation, of loss, of crying; a crash into the most extreme foolishness.

The ritual repeated itself that Sunday with only one definitive, cruel variation. Let us recapitulate: bus, arrival, hike, fallen leaves, Juan Andrés' little feet, police horses, cows behind the fence, Lucía running around, cotton candy, sweets and the playground, of course, the playground with a slide for Lucía and a sand castle for Juan Andrés. The variation, maybe: to have gone with Bernard, a French photographer friend who had the children pose in all imaginable situations.

And a pause, after the hike, in the playground: Magdalena and I speaking with Bernard, Lucía and Juan Andrés playing in the sandbox, Magdalena and I laughing with Bernard on a nearby bench, Bernard who goes to look for a couple of beers, Magdalena who gets up, glances over at the playground and can't believe it: Juan Andrés isn't there, he's not there. The bucket, the shovel, and the sand castle are all there, but he's not, the boy's not there.

Magdalena runs, I run. Magdalena shakes Lucía by her shoulders and asks her where is her brother. "He was there," the girl answers without understanding, "... he was there just a minute ago." But he's not there, he's not there. Magdalena runs over to a police officer. She explains to him screaming. The policeman tries to calm her, he communicates by radio with the other agents in the park, he explains to her that children routinely get lost there. I run to the area of the sweets, to the cotton candy, to the beer stand. Bernard looks in the playground, he detains the nearby people and questions them.

We begin to suspect the people (it must be confessed), we start looking in people's faces. Every single man turns into a disturbed person, a sadist, an assassin. We review every face, every gesture, every garment.

Time passes (they were minutes, maybe, but time itself, memory, tends to dilate them, to spread them out into a substance that continues to be viscous). Juan Andrés doesn't appear: only the bucket in the playground, only his half-finished little sand castle.

We give him up for lost, we cry for him. We curse heaven, humanity, the police, ourselves. We blame ourselves, mutually, we humiliate ourselves.

Saying how and in what moment he appeared wouldn't make any sense (he did appear, actually, licking a strawberry ice cream cone and holding hands with a policeman without understanding why we cried, why we hugged him). The point is what survived of that moment: the unescapable, unrepeatable sensation; the sudden death of a being, love disrupted, torn to pieces; the wound that doesn't heal; tenderness converted into indignation, into hate, into frustration; the fissures between Magdalena and me (we hug and they're there, we kiss and they're there).

It's still, after everything (racing around, the police, all of the consequences), the solitary bucket in the playground, the half-made sand castle.

Black Highway

The day's journey would have a concrete objective: to go as far as Cabo San Román and pass the day on the beach so many friends had raved about: Puerto Escondido.

We had been in Paraguaná for a week, reserving each day for a specific activity: buy crafts in Miraca, swim in El Pico, visit the Arcaya house, admire the church of Santa Ana, go to the salt mines in Las Cumaraguas ... we had been completing all our plans almost religiously.

The sixth day, on the beach of Puerto Escondido, we begin to yield space to the landscape, to the magnetism of the landscape. We had yet to notice the bewitching. Unrecognizable forces had been working on our souls from the first day, since our passage over the isthmus (that ambiguous dimension of having the ocean on both sides of your passage). But later sequences kept adding themselves that were definitively similar: interminable plains of huisaches, thistles, cactus and wind ... a wind that on more than one occasion almost pulled us up by the roots as we went down the road. We weren't the same as before, and it was very late when we came to realize it.

We were, to tell the truth, a troop: Maruja and her three children, Leonor and her two, us and our three. Leaving in the morning was like a military operation: the coolers, the sandwiches, the sodas, the flippers, the fishing reels, the suntan lotion, the towels ... each one demanded something. We traveled in two four-by-four vans.

Cabo San Román was a simple village. We went as far as Puerto Nuevo, we passed Las Cumaraguas, we left behind an old abandoned radio station and, from there on, we oriented ourselves always towards the north on a rocky dirt road. The road brought us close to an irregular coastline of coral formations shaped by the force of disordered currents, down below the high cliffs. The waves crashed aggressively against the shore and raised curtains of water that bathed our windshields. At one point the vegetation suspended itself. Everything seemed almost lunar. Like marks in a fossilized land, lines of coral that sketched all imaginable forms, abrupt breaks in the road (like sudden steps) that our trucks mounted with difficulty. In Puerto Escondido—a grand discovery—we ate turtle soup and lobster. An Italian named Gianni, to our surprise, lifted nets on the beach and we chose from the lobsters that were held captive there.

The children discovered the beach at Puerto Escondido after lunch. They buzzed about like blind flies. They threw aside all the careful planning (buckets, boards, towels, fishing rods) and, with gestures of the possessed, rolled about in the surf. They chased the waves like drunks and hit the crests as though they were challenging the currents. The water, it should be added, was a dull blue, almost transparent: the foam of the waves concentrated more in the center of the bay than towards the sides.

The day trip, I repeat, was executed just as we had envisioned it. Except that on the return—and it's here that the recounting makes sense—Leonor insisted that we must take the other route, the one that follows the western edge of the peninsula.

We left Puerto Escondido behind knowing that our only trail was following the ocean. The geography couldn't fool us and we supposed that, orienting ourselves in relation to the coast, sooner or later we would arrive at the origin of the other highway (Jadacaquiva looked like the nearest outpost of civilization).

Out beyond Puerto Escondido, an unforgettable, grandiose vision: white sand dunes running down to the shore. The kids gathered new energy: they scaled the movable peaks and threw themselves with complete abandon from the pinnacles until they dropped into the ocean. It was a delicious exercise—we must say—and even the adults threw ourselves into the fray. It was a dialectic: cohabiting between water and sand, opting for thesis or antithesis, both infinite and unfinished.

We left the dunes behind (it took some effort to get the vans across on that brief tongue of land which the ocean just barely left open to us) to turn our way onto snaking trails that distanced us and brought us back to the ocean. The landscape became so exact that we almost got dizzy. The landscape was a perfect summary of itself projected exponentially: thistles had never seemed so big to us, huisaches had never seemed so doubled over by the wind, we had never seen so many ephemeral flowers on the creeping cactus, never had we seen such a big billy goat (a real grandfather with a long and pointed beard) orienting his followers and briefly interrupting our passage on what was now for us a cursed deviation.

We began to perceive over the vegetation a tall steel structure that turned out to be the lighthouse at Punta Macoya (we had picked out the point on a map and we recognized it). And afterwards, a few kilometers further down, the route opened up before an endless beach with two houses mislaid in its middle, which turned out to be called (we exchanged a few words with a hermit who came out of one of the shacks) the Ensenada del Pescador.

We lost the children again, it was an endless event. The surface was composed of pools and banks of sand that repeated themselves tirelessly right up to the shore. Each one occupied a sudden swimming pool and crowned himself owner of the puddle as part of a game. There were round pools, ring-shaped ones, oblique, half-moon shaped...

One sequence intrudes into our memory with the force of an anchor thrown into the bed of thought: the brusque breaking of an enormous wave (signs of stronger currents were beginning to appear) and the infinitude of mullet that the whip of water expelled in one stroke onto the sand. The little fish began to arch themselves convulsively to try to reach the pools as best they could, and the children, seeing living plunder before their eyes, set themselves to the task of fishing mullet with buckets, nets, flippers, even their hands. It was exaltation, pure bliss, an encounter with the most unknown. The children in a children's game, determined to take the fullest advantage of the ocean's gift, hunting with the greatest effort little creatures like brilliant silver coins that fought to survive with a demoniac drive: some reached the pools, others slid slippery from the hands of the children in a final wave of their tails, the majority ended up as booty that on that fortunate night adorned our table and calmed our stomachs. Fried mullet melted in our mouths. We held them there for a long time, and even now they still leave a trace on our palates.

We were debilitated. We now looked for a definitive way back. We got back on the road following the same snaking route that distanced us from the ocean and drew us near to it again, and the landscape turned back into the same. It was like a mirage, like a trick, like a trap we were searching for the opportunity to fall into. Nothing indicated to us that we could be advancing (only the sun perhaps, which began to sink towards the right, and the coast itself, re-encountered every now and then).

There comes a moment when the road begins to subdivide; it seems prudent to us to always stay to the right so that we won't distance ourselves too much from the ocean. Except that, precisely, this option begins—we don't know how—to distance us from the ocean. We fell into the trap, into our own trap, into the very deviation we had invented for that specific day trip.

Suddenly we come upon a house, a beautiful earthen house with corrals of goats, and a friendly woman comes out to greet us. "The black highway?" she smiles without teeth. "Keep going down and always to the left," she advises us, not without first picking up one of the babies that pulled on her skirt, "always to the left." It was an order that we obeyed religiously from that moment on.

It got dark. The sun had sunk below the horizon. We had lost the trail of the coast some time before (I think that by now it didn't interest us). Orange, reddish, and purple brush marks began to stain the screen that the sky exhibited to our right. We accelerated, we did nothing but accelerate when we saw that we were losing the light.

A certain fear (huisaches that began to appear ghostly, thistles that reeled like apparitions, the humming of the crepuscular wind that now announced the night) invaded us. The children held in their pee and the two vans jumped over the rocks like creatures fleeing the shadows.

We didn't know how much more time passed. What we do remember is the vision of the black highway: that illusion that fatigue gave us, that finally opened before our anxious eyes. That surface that seemed more inviting than ever, that black accent barely visible in the mouth of what was now darkness, the complicity of the children seeing them all urinate, standing in a row against the purple blanket of the night.

Fissures

Everything is possible under the light of a lamp: from the Chinese shadows to the slow glide of a writing hand. A story arises here and another is aborted. The great pulses are, by definition, those that dominate the scene and impose their judgment while, suspended, the minor pulses await a better moment to recover power in the narrative. The visible, by definition, doesn't convince anybody. We are more interested in the reverse of objects than in that spurious official-dom wherein the whole world tends to recognize itself.

This hand that writes could be the same that extends a greeting to a friend, the same that lights the charcoal of a bonfire, the same that caresses a woman's nervous back, the same that carries a piece of bread to a mouth. At times, even, it's not actually the same one; we could better say that it allows itself to live emulating other hands, and not always friendly ones. The same situations with different actors; the same gestures with different resolutions. It's not a fragile thread that unites the caress of a lover with the blind stubbornness of the assassin.

But let us go, in this case, to the facts: Blanca, my young

wife, has died. The coast guard has found her chalky body in Carenero Bay. There isn't a more foreign scene—at least that's how most people feel—than observing the explosion of a boat with an outboard motor. It's an image—I repeat—that's inconceivable before what a motorboat usually provides: rapid voyages to Puerto Francés, the currents that beat it around Cabo Codera, the transparency of the sandy floor in Caracolito, the bodies like lizards fearless underneath the sun and so many other things. But a motorboat—we must advise—is also full of minor pulses, of hidden structures: the gas line, the cables of the starter, the charges flying from the motor's spark plugs.

I imagine Blanca thrown over the surface of the bow, her body like a dry tongue, her arms oily, her hair thrown about in calculated disorder ... It's a scene that was mine, perfectly mine for many years. The abyss of Blanca's body, yes, our interminable retreats into the small cabin, the rising and falling of our panting, suspended over the oscillation of the waters.

The news of her death has surprised me in the calm of a little hotel in Varenna. The fat reception lady has delivered the telegram and I have to admit I have cried. The pain grows in layers: the telegram announcing this definitive loss has been added to the other loss, this time irrevocable, of only just barely two months ago: Blanca's fresh face telling me no, that everything was over, that she was confused, that the routine was choking her. My arms went towards that face and Blanca turned her head in any direction: toward the kitchen window, toward the magazines in the living room, toward the terrace, toward the ferns on the balcony. Everything can originate in a glance (our encounter, explosive, in a theater, in the dark; the frank laughter, as though of pleasure, as though of acceptance). But everything also vanishes in a glance. The glance is the lock: it's open or it's closed; there is passage or there is no passage.

What's certain is that I live the pain and I review it again and again. I don't know what strange fissure was growing between us, was widening itself (there were weeds in that fissure). Maybe our age difference (fifteen years), maybe our opposite interests ... Blanca announces the decision to me and I break—I must admit it—I break into pieces. I flee, I become delirious, I go adrift. Blanca stays in the apartment alone, inaccessible, strange. Days later, I discover (or some common friend tells me): Blanca has been seen with another man, some guy named Luis, a young playwright, an old friend that she must have re-encountered in that old passion of hers, the stage (because Blanca was seen on stage, she thought she acted on the stage, she lived certain soliloquies with great intensity). And I there watching her (from the beginning) dizzied by the scene, prisoner in a kidnapping, completely submerged in that: the tragedy of another woman who could be (who was, actually) her.

This Luis caresses her (I suppose), kisses her (I suppose), possesses her (I suppose). I don't want to imagine her body next to another's (I can't). I don't want to believe (I can't conceive of it) that the panting could be another's. And it's as if that space were mine alone, as if that land could only respond to my impulses. The unacceptable: to know that the terrain that you have cultivated is now another's; those flowers, that precious garden, those tender fruit, that brief zeal ...

now all of that is in another's hands. It's inconceivable—I repeat.

I had to distance myself. I had to put distance between us. I have now been wandering around the north of Italy for a month, drifting among mountains and lakes like a robot: the peace of Bellagio, the splendor of Cadenabbia, the mustard tint of the sunset in Varenna. I take a ferry on any pretext and land on another stage—always the same. I wish that my story were different, that it were in harmony with what I see: a church, the bell towers, the ancestral houses, the sweet inertia of the lakeshore life. But slowly, bitterly, my story imposes itself on this stage, on any stage. I change the scenery but the piece is always the same.

I suspect that Blanca will make Luis wear the routine that was mine (and this also I can't conceive); the trips to the theater, our weekend escapes to Carenero, our savage panting in the open air, in Caracolito. Luis repeats my story (the story that was formerly mine) and I reserve for myself only the dénouement (which I can't tolerate). It's as if one person were split in two, as if a single role were written for two actors: he, in the beginning, fresh, sucking from that primary spring; I, in the ending, weaving the dark plot of the conclusion.

But I want to take control of my life again (beyond the ghost of Blanca), collect the pieces of my life, reconstruct my mind dissolved in Como Lake, scattered over this black transparency so opposite from the other, the incisive metallic transparency of Puerto Francés.

I was careful before I traveled. A hand takes the car keys, spins the steering wheel interminably before the highway, changes the cassettes in the tape player (a routine that also was ours), shows the membership card in the entrance° to the club, turns on the motorboat's outboard motors so they warm up, twists the steering wheel towards the bay. I let myself be carried away by the immensity of the ocean in a blind, annoying, painful exercise. Traveling without Blanca, traveling without her small figure, traveling without that portable abyss. Nothing made sense—I have to say—neither the bay of Puerto Francés, nor the lukewarm sand of Caracolito, nor the remote port of Chuspa.

I return immediately to another blind, dark exercise. I slap the waves at high speed. I want to run away, I don't know where but I want to run away. I must distance myself from these footprints (ours); I must search for another space, far away, inaccessible. This stage (the apartment, the boat, the bay of Carenero) will be Blanca's but not mine. They can't be mine, they shouldn't be mine.

I reread the telegram and the pain is a growing wound. I was waiting for the notice, sooner or later I was waiting for the notice. It has surprised me here, in Varenna, but it could have intercepted me in any other location, in any other scene. I will walk, I will sleepwalk, through the city all day. I will try to distract myself before any little street, before the outbreaks of plant life in the walls (again the fissures), before the instantaneous moss of the rocks, before the church's punctual bell tower which tries to reorder lives, correct lives.

I leave the hotel, I follow the brief bay and I mount the first ferry that waylays me. The sun falls over Varenna, bathing it in unsuspected colors. I draw away from the fortress, encrusted in the mountain, like someone who leaves a temporary home. I play at deviation and think of the great pulse: the death of Blanca, reviewed in the red pages of the newspapers; Blanca's instantaneous, radical inferno. I don't consider if she would have been with Luis, I ignore whether they will have been reliving some scene that I had once acted. I absolutely wouldn't want to know.

From the ferry I sink into the vision of Varenna—those mustard and red stains that the afternoon sun emphasizes, imposing them on the dark blue of the water in an extreme reflection. And I see my hand, yes, my hand on the ferry's railing, my other hand, the hand of the minor pulses, I see it knotting the gas line to the battery cable on the last trip to Carenero. A short circuit, a sure explosion. I don't want to imagine Blanca's body (I shouldn't imagine it) on top of the water, on top of the quiet water that I now navigate as I pull away from Varenna.

Miraca

One hot afternoon we arrived in Miraca. Ofelia insisted that we enter on an ungraded road, full of big potholes, that, according to a shabby sign at the last intersection, would lead us to the town. Maybe we were wishing we'd encounter wonderful pottery to justify the trip: we had been told of three families dedicated to the profession, with years of tradition.

We didn't choose the best day (nor the best hour). The irregular stretch of road became infinite, and when we finally thought we were arriving, we looked like ghosts. The sky grew into one solid chalky blanket that melted all the clouds; the sun stretched out into a bar of fire that punished the already burned backs; the vegetation was a simulacrum that hid a greater vacuum.

Five, maybe six, houses made up the village of Miraca. Big houses, made of earth, each one with an old huisache tree, with indifferent goats, with round-bellied children playing with the air. The people examine us thoroughly (it's a gaze I haven't forgotten) and they measure each of our actions. Juan, our oldest child, gets out of the car and strolls around without any specific destination; Bernardo, the youngest, becomes enraptured with a large, prehistoric, greenish-red lizard.

Ofelia enters the first of the three houses. A dark parlor receives her and shows her what is for sale. Not much, really. Awkward figures, without any relief work. She enters the second house under the sharp eyes of an austere older woman, dressed in black, her face divided by wrinkles, her gaze turned down.

Only in the third does she find something of interest. The three kings in the shadows. Delineated, firm, green. Ofelia picks up Balthasar and the piece feels heavy in her hands. The face has defined, human features.

Juan had reached a sort of square contained by railings. Something truly surprising. Some yellow flowers grew, isolated, under a constant stream of water. Four concrete benches enclosed the area. And in the center, shrunken, a stone bust of a famous doctor, who came from Miraca. That civic parenthesis floated almost in the middle of a vacuum, like an isolated idea, like something superimposed on the hot geography.

We fled with the three kings (that was our sensation under the collective gaze). Since then we feel that, really, we never discovered Miraca. It's Miraca that discovers us whenever it wants to. At night, when I go to the kitchen to get a glass of water, I cross the living room under the attentive, plural gaze of those three kings.

The Swimmer

Bernardo learned to swim in Puerto Francés. Nela and I observed him looking at the green surface of the water like someone meditating before a transcendental decision. He was standing in the prow of the boat, his arms akimbo, an inflated and phosphorescent life preserver encircling each of his forearms, his gaze lost out towards an unknown point. Those four little years concentrated in such a small body would confront the feat of jumping into the water without any support.

The decision seemed to have been made. Bernardo takes off the life preservers ("the wings," he called them), he leans over the protruding border of the prow, and in one move that we still reproduce in slow motion, he throws himself into the water. He fell on his bottom, his back slightly thrown back, his arms held high. The face that came up out of the surface was that of a playful, lively seal, that hadn't rested at all the whole day. Bernardo splashed with confidence, he moved his little feet beneath the water in precise kicks, and clenched his teeth to the point of breaking his jaw.

We admired him. That evolution didn't pertain to us.

We watched him spin one game into another, one prank into another. We saw him devouring sardines and bread when it was time to improvise a lunch. We saw him in the afternoon fishing with a reel and tugging at the line with his teeth like any Tarzan of the jungle. We saw him collapse exhausted on the light mattress of his cabin like a defeated warrior.

In the wine that accompanied us that night (we irrigated the bloody glasses of our eyes, we became accomplices), Nela and I recreated a scene from five years before. Puerto Francés received us with the same calm of its waters, with its same vertical transparency. We dedicated ourselves to walking along the beach and to making love with fury between the four humid walls of the cabin. There was something to discover beneath the tanned hides, and we admitted to having injured ourselves, to having searched within our flesh for the blood that fed us.

We like to believe that our origins are there, we like to believe that it was then that we gave life to the swimmer.

The Photographer

It could be raining outside; it could just as easily be hot. They're situations that I ignore, to be honest, in this darkroom. My only decoy is this red light bulb that twinkles night and day. The water is ready in the trays and the acids gnaw at the paper to slowly return to me the definitive image of my days.

I began with the night—it was an obsession. The night in all its facets: drunken faces in a discotheque in Las Mercedes, prostitutes on Avenida Libertador, headlights in the rain on a highway, cars in motion, billboards of epileptic neon, the mustachioed face of a bartender in La Candelaria ... until I arrived at what I consider a grand and unique moment: a horse galloping over the El Ciempies overpass, yes, an unexpected image captured at about two in the morning, on my way back home. A lost horse, surely, nervous, a bit angry, not knowing if it should run to one side or the other, and suddenly, under a headlight, almost a spotlight, the horse stops, its eyes breaking out, its neighing vigorous, and I take the photo. The image spread through magazines, exhibitions, catalogues. I repeat, a grand image.

Afterwards there were years of work in the slum of La Ceibita. A different horizon, surely, a different angle on reality: children playing with tires, boys batting bottle caps, a woman leaning against the frame of her doorway, four fat men playing dominoes, an ogre dressed up as a policeman hugging a seventeen-year-old dark damsel (the girl laughs, she laughs and we don't know why), a close close-up of the face of an old woman (more than a face: wrinkles, furrows in the earth), a pig nosing about in the garbage by a stream, a first communion (a white veil against a little girl's face) ... Prizes in Poland, a mention in a contest in Austria, a cover of *Photoplay* magazine.

Two years later, a scholarship takes me to Italy. Then comes what they like to call the "Italian period," a traveling exhibition with two men kissing, a woman dancing with a mask amidst the Carnival in Venice, naked trees in winter, a couple making love on a dock (he's carrying her by the cheeks of her ass, she wraps her legs around him at waist level, and the glance, yes, the glance of the woman that sees the camera from off in another world, in ecstasy), the face of a fisherman in Naples, an anchor tattooed on the colossal arm of a sailor, the momentary face of a model captured in the second that she turns on the catwalk (the white dress, caught in the air, gives the appearance of a spirit abandoning the body), two little girls in a church each with a candelabra (the flames captured in their eyes), a widow in Sicily crying for her dead husband ... A book was published called *Italy: A Vision,* and the magazine *The Photographer* included a special dossier in its anniversary edition.

It's difficult to speak of the impulses, of the themes. I

must admit that it's like a rapture: in the least expected moment it appears like a bite and one has to respond immediately. The course of reality contains mini-sequences, just barely perceptible, states of being that pine for a register, a moment that brings them notoriety. It is as if reality was calling, a beast that calls, that howls before it dies. Yes, photography is like death, the exact instant in which death occurs. Nothing will now be as it is, as it was, as it has remained reflected there, in that precise moment. Like a believer, in the silence of my darkroom, I assist these small, slow, revelations of reality. Revelations that I myself don't measure in the moment of opening the shutter but when the acids recompose for me the precise, initial image—that exact, remote death.

Lately I have been taken by dogs. Anyplace, dogs. Dogs in the middle of the highway, dogs in the street, dogs in the slums, dogs in the restaurants along the beach ... So much abundance also has its inverse: the swollen-up, destroyed, dead dogs. This precise butchery that surrounds us.

I have begun to work on a series of nocturnal dogs. A lot of coffee after dinner and the car rolls itself almost automatically towards the most improbable places. I wander for three or four hours every night. Few eloquent images, difficult to organize. In two weeks of traveling I have only achieved three acceptable photos. The acids reveal them to me briefly: the lost gaze of a brown dog in a mall (a miniature before the shop windows full of fashions), a Dalmatian perched in a fire truck with his tongue out (the animal almost licks the lens), a dog mounting another dog in the Santa Fe township.

This series—tenuous, difficult—has drifted off toward another: I have managed to gather barely ten good photos in months of work. One night I discover everything on the Prados del Este expressway: the impact of an automobile against the ribcage of a street dog offers me all of the edges. The woman driving the car gets out, shocked: the car's metallic grille has gathered bits of the animal. The woman raises her hand to her mouth and she gets back into her car. I captured that precise moment (that death): the woman squatting down to see the dent made by the impact, her hand held to her mouth. The headlights of the car, burning under the rain, add a phantasmal impression to the photo. I thought that this portrait could be the nucleus of the series: tragic, urban, nocturnal. Reality is gathered in bits, in those unknown bits that the night returns to us in the most unexpected places.

The series has robbed me of my drowsiness. It's a new obsession. I feel like it doesn't end, that instead it leads off towards other pathways, each one darker than the last. The series has also confused me. Now I don't know what I'm doing: I merely follow my instincts (the instincts of the series itself). The series is a living creature, that dictates its own pauses and hours, that imposes itself like a definitive, vertical design. I tremble in the solitude of the darkroom: I shiver from the cold (I have slept very little), from the heat, from anxiety. The camera drags me along and I am its slave.

Now I don't want to speak of the images, of the images the acids return to me. They are few, surely, but terminal. I no longer remember, even, when I took them. They appear as if by magic. And I, unknown, enable them, I give them the final bit of life, I suspend them dripping from the clothespins and their dripping is the sweat of the creatures, of the living creatures.

I have thought of a title for the series: *Canines: Friends of Man*. Simple; maybe a bit stupid. *Canines: Creatures of the Night*. Closer, yes, but still imprecise; there's something missing, something that reduces it. I don't want to conceive of it, I can't conceive of it. I return to the images of that night (it's the last certainty that I recall): the woman dismounting from her car, squatting down, her dress under the tenuous rain, the horror of her glance, the bits of animal encrusted in the grille, my voracious eye from the shoulder of the road, my vulgar eye from the shoulder, my insomniac eye watching for the moment, detaining the moment. I knew that was the origin of everything, the nucleus, the reason, the soul.

Since that night I haven't slept, I can't sleep, I mustn't sleep. I'll go out in a few minutes: a new journey waits for me. I will undoubtedly travel the Prados del Este expressway, Santa Fe township, so predisposed, so prosperous in stray animals, misguided, with lost gazes. I accelerate, yes, I know I will accelerate at the sight of any one of them to portray the exact, definitive moment. I have spoken of photography as an action of death, as an epitaph of any death. I corner a dog in my headlights and I hurl the car forward. I hear the impact of the ribcage against the grill. I breathe easier. It's the moment to take a photograph and it could be raining outside.

The Mine

Two words are intimately tied to Germán, my maternal grand-father. One is *bigamist*, the other *republican*. As a bigamist they locked him up on the Canary Islands, upon his return from Cuba (he left, as a matter of fact, a wife and two children on the Caribbean island) to marry Maria Morales, my late grandmother. As an accused republican, he was subjected to a year and a half of jail and allowed limited visits by the family. Inside the four gloomy walls of the dungeon, my grandfather bragged about having read *Don Quijote*, from which many years later he recited complete passages to us between the corncakes, meat and potatoes of successive meals.

The family has charged itself with fattening the legend and now we no longer know how much of it is true. To tell the truth, it doesn't matter much to us. We undoubtedly prefer the splendor of myth to earthly simplicity.

Years later, from Havana, his Cuban daughter visited us in Caracas; a sixty-year-old woman, sweet and miserable, who presented memories that weren't ours: she spoke of a rigid man, rarely seen, who worked from sunup to sundown in the fields, and who, for unexplainable motives, left the house

one day to never return. A school in one of the Cuban prov-
inces, the woman assures us, bears her brother's name (my
grandfather's other child), a national hero fallen in arms in
1957 whose memory the Revolution wanted to preserve.

I shouldn't have a name since the day I met my grandfather (it's the image I want to retain). I should be nothing but
the ten-year-old child, disobedient and ethereal, whom my
grandfather adopts and re-educates in a matter of days. My
grandfather erases our names and introduces us into another
world: the world of the Mine, a small ranch on the outskirts
of La Laguna that became the refuge of his final days.

The Mine—we came to discover it as adults—was barely
a tongue of land. It was almost nothing. But under the guid-
ance of my grandfather (the gaze that lost itself following the
smoke from his pipe) we escaped from the world eating straw-
berries, figs, grapes, climbing up to the pine trees on the hill
(it was an interminable walk), looking for shade under the
grapevine that took possession of the terrace (it was our lead
soldier's refuge), swimming in a pond that was always half
full, where we rolled over and over until reaching the fullness of fatigue.

With firm and grumbling mastery, with schedules and
sequences that today we still pine for, Grandfather reserved
the tool room for the end of the day. A humid pit, with an
odor somewhere between rancid and vegetal, in which we
always imagined a gold excavation (what else could be hid-
ing under the name The Mine?). My grandfather always let
us enter in the afternoons, our bodies worn out from the
pond, and those plowing tools hanging from the stone walls
invariably seemed to us to presage an excavation, the mys-

tery of a task which my grandfather reserved for himself in his most secret hours. Any trade underground, the mouth of any tunnel (no matter how small it might be), opened up the route to gold, and there was more than one who swore he had encountered the brilliance of a sparkling grain as the night was falling.

My cousins inherited the Mine and they ended up renting it. They tell me that during La Laguna's airport tragedy (two jumbo jets crashed in the fog and scattered nine hundred corpses all over the area), the Mine functioned as the center of operations from which ambulances, police patrols and fire trucks were coming and going all night long.

Today, every time I go out on an excursion with my children, the vision of a pine-covered hill awakes a secret passion in me: I then let the gaze of the grandchild that I still am run over it, and search among the pits in the ground for the rancid odor of gold.

The Island

I see an island. In fact, I have always seen it. The island is like a mountain encrusted into the middle of a lake of dark waters. It rains on the island, it has always rained. And from any point along the coast of the lake, the island is barely perceptible. A blanket of fog preserves it from the gaze of humanity.

The island is blanketed with vegetation: pine, birch, chestnuts. There isn't a bit of land that is free from the explosion of greenery. The water slowly bathes the shores and now even these extremities of the land are fertile: moss or lichens cover the rocks.

The island is more visible under a full moon. But, obviously, the fog impedes every view. We see just barely the peak, a higher island floating above the blanket of clouds.

Nobody has tried to cross the lake towards the island. It's a challenge which nobody takes. They prefer to see it from faraway, mysterious and unattainable, and imagine anything they desire on it. Imagine, for example, a secret, unsuspected civilization, to which no one has access. These are the legends that the island itself has gradually nourished.

The island survives all changes, all storms. The lake frequently harbors violent storms bringing lightning that lights up the island's night with a precision that only shifting clouds navigate.

The possibility that someone could live on the island is ignored. As far as this goes, everything is mere speculation.

Years ago I became bored with the island, unchangeable, and I have preferred to examine the various shores of the lake. There are flat sandy shores; there are abrupt coasts of black cliffs; there are mountains whose slopes fall into the water, drowning their overflowing vegetation.

Nobody comes to the island because nobody has seen it. I have inhabited it for years and I can assure you that I have not seen any sign of life on the rest of the lake. My passion has grown so that today I spread myself out on the other shores and try to imagine someone navigating towards the island. It's the exercise that I cultivate, it's the task that I have set myself to fulfill some day: arrive on the island, encounter me on the island, give this ancient shipwreck a propitious resolution.

— *for Patricia Guzman*

Losses

Carla doesn't retain—that's what the doctors diagnose. She invariably gets pregnant and then, upon completing the first five months, loses the baby. She has tried everything, all in vain: *in vitro* fertilization, staying in bed, retentive girdles, fertility pills.

Carla has now lost four. Together with her husband she has cried over each of them (more or less intensely) in relation to the number of months. The losses have also affected the furniture in the house: cradles that haven't been rocked, little tubs without water, baby clothes that have been given away to friends.

Now the family doesn't dare to do anything: you can't blindly bet on the future only to find yourself stuck holding the gifts.

The last loss fell upon two five-month-olds ("the twins," Carla called them). The doctors treated her with the greatest care and announced a happy ending. Carla wakes up one morning with clots of blood between her legs and the whole family falls into mourning.

Since then, Carla and her husband have given up. They

have returned to a simple domestic life and they have tried to re-inject the dynamism of the old days into their activities. But one room in the house remains under lock and key: the twins' room.

Moonlit

From the beginning there were four of us: Alexandra, Rodrigo, Nela and me. The idea of crossing the island grew slowly along the length of the stony bay of Los Cristianos Beach, between mugs of German beer and a liquor called "malmsey wine" that barely left a sweet aftertaste on our palates. The days elapsed beneath the lazy inertia that we had anticipated: Rodrigo with his photography, Alexandra with her Spanish magazines, Nela looking in shop windows at bikinis and me bottled up in a book of science fiction.

The arrival at Los Cristianos—a bus from the airport left us and our luggage in front of the hotel—didn't surprise us too much. The brochures we received in Caracas had advanced us a few images: successive hotels bordering the bay, large commercial zones, fast food restaurants and a few bars that we later would visit. Maybe from all of that identification we retained the impression that Los Cristianos was like a brush stroke of white paint spread across the black rocky background that the ancient lava had turned silent.

It was difficult to escape from the influence of the volcanoes in Tenerife. Everything—every step we took, every establishment, every tourist guide—presaged the volcanoes. Rodrigo and I (the women, bored by our exploratory zeal, had gone to the beach) managed to view in the hotel a documentary on the last eruption of a volcano, filmed at the southern extreme of the island of La Palma. It impressed us beyond measure: the lava flowed down through improvised trenches and reached the ocean sending up mile-long columns of steam. A truly maritime boiling, of unimaginable proportions, that in seconds turned the fishes' cold water into the inferno of a pressure cooker. Volcanologists spoke in the documentary and affirmed that with this new eruption the "beautiful island" had stolen miles of land from the sea. Black, sterile land; burned land, it must be said, which the farmers observe with suspicion since they can't imagine even a sprig of vegetation for centuries.

Captivated by the images, Rodrigo and I caught up with the women on the beach to display our expertise for them. I think it was there, upon the black sand that the sea licks with its transparent tongue (again the presence of the volcanoes), that the idea of crossing the island to the other side began to gestate. The route would take us along the southern slope to El Teide (which was what Rodrigo and I wanted), the central volcano of the island and the highest peak in Spain, and then drop us along the northern slope toward little villages full of local color. We fixed a Friday for the excursion (it was Tuesday when we decided), and Rodrigo and I agreed to handle the preparations. Basically we took charge of renting a small car (it turned out to be a red Volkswagen Bug) and packing sandwiches, fruit and water for the road.

The two days before the journey stretched themselves out. The girls continued sunning their bodies, Rodrigo tried to penetrate the texture of some cliffs with his lens, and I progressed in my novel with a certain disenchantment (in the disorder of my reading I had barely retained the name of a certain Aldrin, the explorer of a lunar colony). We amused ourselves in the afternoons playing cards and recounting the stories of mutual friends in Caracas. The night before the excursion—clear, unforgettable—we ate wrinkled potatoes, a traditional island dish. Alexandra passed her tongue over her salty lips and I wanted to believe that image disturbed Rodrigo. The early morning hours caught us walking along the edge of the beach (yet again the black sand) telling stories that doubled the women over with laughter. The full moon created a mobile reflection in the water that ventured onto the land where brilliant particles recomposed it with difficulty (I thought of Aldrin). By this time the wine had risen to our heads and I seemed to see Rodrigo's hand intercepting Alexandra's over the frail light that the sand reflected.

Friday received us with an omnipresent light. We wanted to leave early (the VW Bug purred in front of the house) so we wouldn't have to rush through the most interesting passages. We slowly ascended through the towns and neighborhoods that the road planted before our eyes. There were country stares, red-cheeked children, men with black vests and berets, furrows of black earth growing potatoes, carrots, beets. A town's labor stopped us in the middle of the route: trucks maneuvering before a harvest while the whole town threw itself into extracting the potatoes, putting them in sacks and mounting them on the trucks that were arriving and departing. Green meadows overtook wastelands, low stone walls, three or four goats that seemed lost to us. The swollen udder of a cow (retained in the foreground by Rodrigo's lens) that, fearless, chewed the grass in the middle of the road; she withdrew carrying the milk in a bouncing dance under the trumpeting (or whistling) of the Bug's horn.

We left the earth behind, the fertile earth, to enter into gritty lace, almost vertical, totally covered by enormous pine trees. And at this point out springs a comment from Rodrigo (something he read in a guide in the hotel) about the great climatic difference between the two sides of the island. The south slope (across which we were ascending), completely dry since the days when the Spaniards cut down all the trees to build the ships that took them to America, has been re-planted with pine trees that perpetuate the acidity of the soil. The north slope, more prone to intercept the air currents that arrive filled with water vapor, is moistened by every cloud that caresses it, and fine springs grow forth that sprinkle the land with a more varied vegetation.

The pine trees gradually block our vision as well as our sense of smell. The repeating trunks and green branches like hanging brooms begin to vibrate in our retinas (some kinetic effect, no doubt). At the beginning of what seemed like motion sickness, Alexandra thinks she sees a lookout constructed around an enormous pine tree. We stop the Bug and get out to catch our breath. A wooden sign, nailed to the trunk of the biggest pine tree, singles it out as the oldest tree on the slope. Alexandra, Nela and I try in vain to circle it with the human chain formed by our arms. Rodrigo saves a sequence of the drama: in the first photo Alexandra and Nela are holding hands, in the second me and Nela embracing half the trunk, in the third I am spreading my arms and legs from the other side, the final one features the generous yard between Nela's hand and mine (each of us stretched to the limit) trying fruitlessly to reach one another.

The view from the lookout was a summary of our days. On the most distant line of the horizon was the ocean (a blue and misty tongue): on the next line, more in the middle, the white stripe of Los Cristianos; on a third line, closer and duller, the successive neighborhoods of the road (green, brown, and white planes); and, finally, almost at our feet, the skirts of the mountain we had just climbed, covered with pines.

According to Rodrigo's map we should be getting close to the summit by now. We left behind the last pine trees (thinner, more tenuous) to encounter extensive and disorderly rocky surfaces. We didn't visualize it until a curve threw the Bug into the new scenery. It was a valley of rocks, lunar, an infinite valley of rocks (and again I thought of Aldrin) that extended across the full width of our view. The most distant view brought us light red, purplish, and greenish tones; the ground closer to us was gray, black, white, coal-colored, chalk-colored. It was an ocean of lava: ancient, silent, petrified. It was a distant, constant, self-duplicating ocean.

We stopped along the side of the road. Each of us let ourselves be carried along by our own pulse; subjected to the extreme cruel liberty of the landscape. We saw Rodrigo climb off the right edge of the road (an angle maybe, searching for an angle); Alexandra stood up leaning on the Bug as if she were submerged; Nela and I entered the valley, jumping carefully from rock to rock. It didn't smell like anything (or it smelled like everything?). After escaping the cloying scent of the pine trees, this smelled like nothing. The air was pure (so pure that it burned). It was hard not to imagine that minute rocks were entering our lungs, invisible particles spinning across time. The silence was central, deaf to itself, barely interrupted by a certain humming, the air searching for its origin, trapped for centuries between the rock walls of the valley, insomniac in its boredom.

Rodrigo felt that photographs were useless. He tried angles, focuses; nothing satisfied him. Suddenly, flipping the focus on the camera from one extreme to the other, he crashed into Alexandra's image (gray sweater and black pants against the red stain of the Bug). He likes the angle and he presses the shutter. But nothing more. His gaze gets lost following the channels of lava, the tentacles of a grounded octopus that unfurls its extremities to the full length of all imaginable space. He continues absorbed in the furrows of the earth and raises his gaze to encounter a limpid virginal sky with barely a thread of clouds—mere traces that dissipate.

Nela begins to collect stones and throw them in a basket. The first impression is like that of touching coal—big rocks that weigh very little. She touches the soft texture of a rock (there is no dust whatsoever) and feels that the center is petrified. The colors mutate; behind coal-black comes the chalk-white, comes a gray, out jumps an emerald green, dilates a ferrous brown ...There are pores in the rocks (now he sees them), pores like bubbles, bubbles frozen in time, infernal vapors that have remained imprisoned like a choked scream. I feel that the rocks perspire, have perspired for centuries, and that they are only the residue of a great combustion.

It was difficult to separate ourselves from the place, and that was only the first impression. The silence grew among us (it was a slow wave that rose through the chest) and floated in the car. A slow sharp cold also began to enter through the windows. The landscape didn't change, rather it repeated itself, it sank, it exposed its own great definitive nudity. The landscape undressed itself, yes, it did nothing but undress itself. The car advanced following the only distinct element in the scene: the serpentine road in the middle of the ocean floor.

Suddenly, on the left-hand margin, like a pinnacle, like a vertical scar on the horizon, the peak of El Teide. The volcano drew straight up to its apex in one clean line, in a single stroke that ended in its open, snowy, mouth. A plume of smoke, barely perceptible, loosened itself from what must be the crater and disputed with the two strands of clouds the canvas of the background of the sky. El Teide was the color of sharkskin and the crown of snow looked singed at its highest edge, with black specks. The more we advanced—always following the sinuous valley—the more omnipresent it became. We wanted to imagine its crater from the cabin of the Bug— a cauldron barely bubbling—and we tried to reach the remote past when its tellurian fury virtually arrested the whole island with slow tongues of fire that threw themselves burning into the ocean.

Now on the slope of the volcano, just at the point where the road crossed its base, we stopped again. Nela added to her collection of dead rocks, Alexandra scaled a crag, and Rodrigo followed a branch of dry lava that lost itself again in the valley. Here the landscape turned bipolar: to the north the base of the volcano, to the south, the spits of perfectly formed land, the arms of earth that remained quiet and dry just as they had cooled. They were the open veins of the volcano, the blood of that human creature whose peak was still breathing the fatigue of centuries, its millennial expiration, the magma pulled from the center of the earth and exposed to its extreme mortal sacrifice.

I wanted to separate from the group, venture along a branch of land that crossed the highway to lose itself in the center of the valley in a sinuous, serpentine route. I wanted to think of Aldrin; yes, I wanted to recall the only sequence of the novel that I could remember. I saw Aldrin hiking with his heavy boots and his illuminated spacesuit through a so-called Sea of Tranquility. I saw him being subjugated by the rocky massifs that, like vertical knives, abruptly dissected the lunar valley. It was his first excursion outside the colony and the narrator distracted himself by describing the landscape. Advancing like a blind man, letting myself follow the string of rocks, I made Aldrin think of the woman he had left behind on earth, when he confronted his mission. Their last meeting had been in a strange place, a rocky place, and Aldrin remembered the snowy form of that naked body, as though it were calling him, against the black field of a rock. As I lifted my steps I thought I saw for the last time the reflection of the cliffs on Aldrin's illuminated spacesuit, and I thought that the moon upon which I now walked was the same that bathed that entranced body in its light, the body that had waited for me on a rocky bed and had tinged all of my skin.

Madams

We went to El Callao and we saw nothing. Only agitated, drunk, half-naked people, celebrating Carnaval.

They had told us of a brilliance that didn't exist anymore, of a local color, of a buried tradition of which not even the air preserved a trace.

On the central avenues the jewelers dedicated to the region's gold were closed with steel bars and shutters.

The people were all concentrated in large, sweaty parades that advanced along a few streets presided over by a car loaded up with enormous speakers. They were human serpents that evolved blind under dry, blaring, repetitive music.

We took refuge in the Plaza Bolivar: a concrete esplanade, a glorious civic project, dirty and full of garbage where the hordes had passed just minutes before.

All of a sudden a ray of sunlight illuminated them seated on a bench in the plaza: isolated, meticulous, old by now, three elegant madams communicating in patois beneath the black and smiling hue of their faces.

Lakes

Just like the water they contain, lakes flow and recompose themselves in my memory. There are big ones that cannot be embraced, open-mouthed like estuaries; there are also little ones, short, designed as ponds or contained by dams. There's a secret sympathy with lakes, a broken knot. Something that hints at a primitive life in which we surely swam happily like coelacanths through the dark waters of history.

A first lake is Maracaíbo's. There I am with Hernán fishing for needlefish. Every afternoon an abandoned drilling tower set about thirty feet from the shore in Lagunillas awaited us. You had to stride with great balance along a half-rusted pipe that joined the tower to the coast. Of course, entrance was forbidden. But the influence of the needlefish was stronger than the sworn obedience to our mothers. Some ordinary afternoon I see Hernán stroll along the pipe on the way back. In a moment of carelessness he spins over himself (the tube being the axis of his body) until he's barely hanging on by his hands. I couldn't help in time. And to tell the truth, he didn't hold on very long; the briny, oily, polluted water welcomed him. It took us a while to get the oil stains out of his clothes (it was an almost useless effort), to later receive his mother's punctual scolding.

Another sequence also occurred on Lake Maracaíbo and it had to do with fishing trips that Juan Andrés's father organized. Certain Saturdays we went in a speedboat from the port of Lagunillas out into the lake (we couldn't see land from the fishing spot) and there the curvina was our celebration. We caught thousands of them—big, robust, curious—and there were so many that we saved them in the freezer for days. Here I remember in a special light all of Juan Andrés's father's efforts to teach us the fine art of fishing. Everything was measured: the bait, the pull, the tension of the line, the position of our hands on the rod, the way in which we threw out the line, the signs one had to use to confuse the fish once it bit ... Everything responded to a wise physics that we felt was foreign to the free whim of the lake.

A third episode, also lacustrian, rescues me in the clinic in Bachaquero with the burning pain of appendicitis. The diagnosis seemed definitive and Dr. Godoy, the attending physician, recommended that they rush me to a hospital in Maracaíbo. I remember precisely the nocturnal crossing with my father (I went lying down and dizzy from pain in the car's back seat) and the ferry that waited for us at midnight to cross the narrowest stretch of the lake at Palmarejo. All the effort was in vain; Dr. Godoy had been mistaken in his diagnosis, and now all the way over in Maracaíbo, they treated me for simple indigestion with sedatives. My father stopped playing dominoes with Godoy on Saturday and I stopped saying hello to his daughter Irene.

Since then there have been successive, numerous lakes,

small in size, and ungenerous at the hour of retaining images. There is the one in Valencia, seen now from my Uncle Delio's melon field (I was shocked to find so many snails in this fertile land). There's the Guri reservoir and the clear memory of the moment when they closed the gates and began to fill the dam: the animals gathered on the peaks of the hills fleeing the water, and they managed to save boas, capable of twisting completely around a man, that for hours resisted the mechanical wires. There's also the Camatagua reservoir, where we admired the tricolor stripe of a recently caught Peacock fish.

From lakes I conserve the tranquility of their waters, that immensity so different from the ocean. A wise calm, conscious of its movements and its limits. One can consult with these waters and design all kinds of mechanisms to connect their shores: tour boats, ferries, sailboats, speedboats.

I have tested it one more time coming to Lake Como, this mass of dark water that rests at the foot of the Alps. I awake day after day before its waters and confirm that nothing has changed. There are, of course, sinuous clouds, passages of water, electric storms that generate a few ringlets on its surface. Nothing to fear, nevertheless.

I discover that this could be any lake. The slow tide of its water recreates Hernán's fall in Lagunillas, the curvina waving its tail in the air, the point of pain in that midnight ferry, the melons of Valencia, the Peacock Fish in Camatagua, and the Andean trout.

In all of them I have fished, certainly, and I have also been the one fished by all of them.

The Wait

The man opens the razor and closes it again. He leans out on the balcony. Still, nobody on the street. He returns to the rocking chair with the newspaper. He reads about the murder of the Italian woman. He stops and looks at the ceiling: peeling from the humidity. He gets up. He goes to the bathroom. His face buries itself in the water his palms hold. He looks in the mirror: his face wearing three days of stubble. It's useless, he thinks, everything is useless. He returns to the rocking chair, and picks up the newspaper. There's the photo of the Italian woman: young, beautiful, strange circumstances.

He's tired. He knows he's tired. He tries lighting a cigarette. The first puff burns his throat. He's thinking, tries to think. But he can't manage to concentrate. Can't do it. Doesn't know what to do. One possibility is not to wait any more. Go down to the street and not wait. Another is to fortify himself with patience and keep himself alert.

He returns to the balcony, sees the lake in the distance, the headland in the middle of the lake, the country house. The morning passes quietly, silently. Only small maneuvers in the port, cars entering and leaving a ferry. The water looks serene. He doesn't understand why he's so uneasy, why so impatient.

The man opens the razor again. He sees the metallic blade, it tempts him. He closes it again. He walks around, he crosses the small studio. He returns, he wants to return to the articles about the Italian woman in the newspaper. It's just that reading bothers him too, it makes him anxious. He concentrates, tries to concentrate. He sees the black and white photo of the Italian. He sees the mouth, those thick eyebrows, the abundant hair. He can't explain it.

He's hungry, a dry hunger that rises in his esophagus with cramps. He looks for the bag, knowing it contains two cheese sandwiches, a piece of cake, a peach, a bottle of seltzer water. He picks up the peach and feels it. He searches for the razor to cut it, but no, he doesn't want to cut it. He believes he shouldn't cut it with the razor. He looks for something else, anything else. Finally he bites it: a big generous bite. The pulp melts in his mouth. The flavor is ambiguous, yes: it's sweet but leaves a bitter aftertaste in his mouth. Again he bites the meatiness that surrenders beneath his teeth. He sucks on the pulp, he contemplates it, as if he wanted to extract juice, as if there were a secret hidden there. Afterward come the sandwiches. He doesn't like whole wheat bread but this time he tolerates it. He chews slowly, bored, lazily. He thinks of a cow, yes, he thinks of a cow and his appetite disappears. He leaves the sandwich half-eaten. The other one he doesn't even try. Then he tries the cake. It's a fruitcake, yes. One, two bites, and he abandons it too.

Again he goes out on the balcony. Still nobody on the avenue. Back to the bathroom. He urinates a thick, yellow, fetid stream. There he is in the mirror. He thinks of shaving. That could be a possibility: shaving. But he's afraid someone will arrive while he's shaving, they'll arrive on the avenue, come looking for him. He rejects the possibility of shaving. It's useless, he thinks, it's useless.

He returns to the balcony and lets his eyes wander off over the lake. The headland and the country house are still there. He returns to the rocking chair, the newspaper, the Italian woman. He tries to finish the murder story: a dry razor cut in the abdomen, a hemorrhage. He stops, looks at the razor, not knowing why he opens it. He doesn't know why he compulsively cleans it with the napkin that held the sandwich. He sees the face again: the eyes, the thick eyebrows, the way he knows her, the way he'd like to know her.

He throws himself against the back of the rocking chair, lets his muscles relax. He lets himself get carried away on a slow drift. He feels tired, but he can't sleep. He returns to the bathroom. More water in his eyes. Lots of water in his eyes. He returns to the chair: he wants to see the Italian woman, trace her details one more time, lose himself in that enigma, in that inactivity.

It occurs to him to write, of course, to leave a note explaining. That will be enough, he thinks, that would prevent any misunderstanding. It's just a possibility. He thinks that then he could go down to the avenue, walk along it, buy a magazine. He writes the note: a scribble. He looks for the razor: opens it, closes it again. He puts it in his pocket. He's going to open the door, he's going out on the street. But no, he'd better not, he thinks. He turns back, picks up the note and crumples it up. It's better not to leave a trail, no clues at all, he thinks.

Back to the chair, then he gets up. returns to the balcony. He wants to lose himself in the Italian woman's face, lose himself out on the headland in the lake. No one will come, he thinks, no one will ever come. No one has to come. He's tense, he abandons himself, loses his fear, looks for another piece of paper. This time, yes, he thinks, the note, the explanation. He writes the first phrase: another scribble, he scratches out the writing. He thinks and lets himself relax, he doesn't know how but he lets himself relax. He sees himself with the Italian woman on the peninsula. He wants to love the Italian woman in the country house on the peninsula. He tries to get deep into that face, tries to describe it, to possess it. He feels relaxed, he penetrates into the face of the Italian and he feels relaxed. He advances, he moves through a tunnel, a spinning whirlwind. He knows that after making love to her in the country house on the headland he has to invent a death for the Italian woman, he has to press the razor into her torso. Desperate, possessed, he lets his emotions flow, he lets the scribble grow, he lets the writing pour slowly out of his hand and he describes the last encounter with the Italian woman. Now he sees himself walking toward the headland and he knows that nobody will come to look for him.

Extension of the Flesh

My grandfather Antonio wasn't much. Just barely a starched white shirt, with a stiff collar and crisp cuffs. Everything could be white when I think of Grandfather, everything could be a great white stage. His conduct, that permanent silence. An emotional life that came out in torrents, I always assumed; or a vacant life, maybe, a life without any depth.

I can't see white rice without seeing Grandfather, I can't eat roast beef without imagining him. Manners were measured, planned. My grandfather cut the roast passing his knife through one of the gaps in his fork so as not to lose equilibrium, the pulse. It's a devastating image: the knife guiding itself through one of the slits in the fork.

Some of the blood from the roast beef bathes the rice. It was a slow flood, again measured. It wasn't a generous stream of sauce flowing over the mound of rice, no. It was an approximation, a pact. I sat down to watch him eat, just that simply, I sat down with my elbows on the table and I watched him eat. He ruminated, my grandfather, I can say that he ruminated.

Everything else was predictable: the job in the hardware

store (he was the bookkeeper), the newspaper, the club sandwiches that he brought to Maria Victoria (my capricious aunt),
his evening trips to the store on the corner.

The arrival of the grandchildren on vacation transformed
his routine, embellished it. We caught a green bus in San
Bernardino that took us downtown. My grandfather made us
visit all the monuments (the Pantheon, Plaza Bolivar, Plaza
San Jacinto, the Liberator's House), tuned to a recital that
he refined with each visit. The explanations on the last tours
were never the same as those on the first. On the last ones
there was more information as well as more enthusiasm.

One ritual was unforgettable: the horse and buggy ride
through the streets of San Bernardino. An old man gave the
ride and my grandfather visited him every time we arrived,
usually for Christmas. The wagon advanced slowly over streets
that seemed cobblestoned to me. I can evoke the exact sound
of the beast's hoofs and I understand why even today that
tapping still disturbs me. I hear the clip-clop of any horse
and I know that I'm with my grandfather.

His last days—after they had retired him from the hardware store—weren't his best. He bottled himself up in the
newspaper from early morning on (I'm afraid he even read
the masthead), and late in the afternoon we would see him
folding those printed sheets to suddenly lecture us on any
topic: politics, economics, history (his preferred subjects). I
always had the feeling that I never talked to my grandfather
enough (I think he also had that feeling, I think he was
waiting for me to the end of his days). And I carry that
sensation like a package, and that sensation never dilutes
itself at all.

My grandfather died when I was seventeeen and living in Caracas. I visited him very rarely, really, I was submerged in other things like any adolescent. I am carrying him still in my arms (his body wasn't much anymore) to take him to the Medical Center. It was the last time I saw him and he asked me about two of my closest friends. The next dawn found him breathless: a stream of hot blood had run down his trachea. My grandfather breathed blood (the blood of the roast beef, I thought). It was the last thing he did in life.

— *for Violeta Rojo*

Mother of Pearl Bridge

Papa has had aquariums all his life. It has been one of his few constants, it has been an obsession. In Punta Cardón, in Bachaquero, in Maracaíbo, in Lagunillas, in The Hague, in Caracas ... every point along our journey has cultivated an aquarium. They have been vertical, round, portable, built-in ... every possible shape, I imagine, defining the eras of our lives. Thus, a built-in aquarium gave a sense of permanence, of stability, while a portable one (the one I was able to improvise in my room) meant that a new move was not far in the future.

The aquariums have also expressed the health of the family, its well-being. A well-maintained aquarium, its filters working, its carbon purified, has always been the sign of harmony; an aquarium abandoned, on the other hand, the dead fish floating, the water below the appropriate level, the glass dirty and with moss growing on it, has evidenced our problems, our trials.

Among the many senses that they preserve, I retain a double lesson regarding aquariums. The first is external and has to do, fittingly, with shape. From the grand variety of fish (kissing fish, zebras, half-moons, swordfish, catfish, boring old goldfish ... a whole vocabulary to invent, a whole genealogy) to the whole unlimited universe of what we could call their technical implements: the filter, the cotton for the filter, the carbon, the sand, the little rocks, the artificial or natural seaweed, the constant bubbling that oxygenates the water, the food. A whole ecosystem, neat, delicate, demanding, that must be watched day and night, if we don't want a fish to become unhinged and begin biting the others.

The other lesson is internal; it's the one that has to do with the background of things, with intimacy. What the aquarium says about us, about our concentration, about our commitment, about our dedication. We could be the fish in the aquarium, and each bit of healthiness also reveals our own condition.

To recapitulate the number, the shapes, the variations of the aquariums would be a useless, difficult and painful exercise. It would be like reconstructing our own life, like remaking our own footsteps. I long for the commitment invested in the construction and mounting of the aquariums and I deplore when they fall into disuse, when we have abandoned them. In their waters are, biting their own tails, life and death: the same cycle of life, of our own lives.

The images are innumerable: from seeing fish giving birth to seeing fish killing one another with their violent jaws, from seeing the chromatic inertia of a Japanese Warfish to understanding the fear of the half-moon, from seeing a goldfish swallowing and throwing out grains of sand (an exercise that always seemed to me to be close to cleanliness, to the protective) to seeing the catfish traverse the floor of the aquarium cleaning up the other fishes' waste (another act of sanitation). Thus are the fish; thus are our lives.

Every trip to the beach, every journey to the mountains, turned into a perfect pretext for fabricating or refining aquariums. The seaweed from Borburata went into the aquarium, the rocks from Adícora as well, not to mention the coral from Chichiriviche. Papa had to filter all the dirt and select the useful. From this whole inventory only one piece has survived—strange, deformed, it's almost an amulet.

I found it in Paraguaná, on Tiraya beach. The white sand of Tiraya hides treasures. Since everything is white, the dissimilar stands out all by itself. I walked along looking for little rocks (for the aquarium, of course) and a sudden glare hit my eyes. It was a bit of conch shell, undoubtedly. It seemed a bit like an oyster, but also had some snail elements. Arching over itself, smooth on one face and wrinkled on the other, the piece was in the form of a C. It was pointless to search for its precise origin: we thought of mollusks, shells, clams. The exterior part of the C was all of mother of pearl (a gradation that went from silver to rose); the interior part, a greenish brown color. I took the discovery to Papa (it was one of our first aquariums, the one in Punta Cardón, and I was only four years old) and the piece kept his interest as well.

The piece became everything: the little catfish's den in Bachaquero, the ledge on which the goldfish scratched itself in Maracaíbo, the wall with which the corroncho camouflaged itself in Lagunillas, a living sculpture to which no fish dared draw near in The Hague, and finally a little bridge under which passed all the species (of the successive aquariums) in Caracas. And that's how we have preserved it right up to today, as a bridge, as a mother of pearl bridge.

The piece is still there, in today's aquarium, in my Papa's house. I see it every now and then, I bump into it every now and then. From Tiraya to Caracas, I think, a whole life concentrated in this piece of shell. At times it revels in health (when Papa sets himself to changing the filters and the fish glow and swim with energy) and at times I find it dark and forgotten (when nobody maintains the aquarium and the dirtiness begins to blur the clarity of the water). But it's always there, day and night, in cleanliness and in filth, the only piece which has survived everything, all the fish, all our habits, all our forces, and all our forgetfulness.

I wanted to recapture this amulet of my first four years, of my whole life. But I think that it's too late now. I'll live, I'll return home, I'll die, and there'll always be a fish beneath the mother of pearl bridge.

— *for Blanca Strepponi*

Spoken Portrait

It's hard to believe that things are as they are. It's hard to believe it. At times I don't feel like I'm anybody. Let me explain: At times I feel like I'm only what I see. Nothing surprises me more than a mirror (or a photo): suddenly it reveals my presence, my existence. Then I recognize, immediately, that I am someone, that I'm not only seeing, but that I am also seen.

And then there's nothing better than walking alone through a park, down any side street, around a fountain, looking at things, the movement of things, things resting. I am in what I see (that would be the formula). A kind of omniscient glance, yes, we could say almost celestial, that I pour out over everything (or that spills out as I stroll distractedly). Obviously all of this gets upset when I discover the reverse of reality: the fact that I am also seen, that I can also be the victim of someone who is proceeding exactly like me.

These reflections spring from something that recently happened to me. I can summarize it roughly. One Friday, at five in the morning, I had to travel to Valencia on business. The trip had been marked in my calendar for days. Thursday night I arrive home tired, I eat, and it occurs to me to check the van, to have it completely ready in the morning. Just the essential things: gasoline, air in the tires, motor oil. Upon raising the hood I discover that I'm missing the battery cap (the guy who parks cars at some restaurant or garage must have taken it: a common practice in Caracas). I look at the motor and, imagining the acidic liquid somersaulting along the whole highway, I know that I must find a replacement at all costs.

Where can I find a battery cap at eight on a Thursday night? The only place I can think of is a fix-a-flat place on Solano Avenue, a little beyond Chacaíto, where I landed one night with a flat tire. I seem to remember seeing a sign that announced it was open twenty-four hours, so I ask Julieta to accompany me on this trivial journey. We cross the city from La Urbina and, upon arriving, we see that the garage door has already closed. A light inside makes me think that maybe there's still someone there and I ask Julieta to check.

It's here that everything turns inside out, here that I stop being the habitual observer of things. I would rather have entered this sequence from the other side, from the aggressor's perspective, and said something like, "We've got some hot dates tonight and we need the van." But it's a sequence that evades me. I then try to locate myself on another plane, maybe on the perspective of an omniscient observer, to short-cut through the situation. I want to say that I'm not the victim; I want to become the narrator in this story, I want to see myself from a distance.

I feel a pistol against the left side of my ribcage (the man feels it, without a doubt). Yes, this will be the beginning of the story: I feel the gun in my ribs and I realize that they have opened the van door (I looked at Julieta talking to the mechanic who had come out to help her). I feel the revolver in my ribs and the man (it's a boy about twenty years old) presses it against my bones indicating that I better move into the back. I do it immediately and, in the same movement, two more young men get in: one climbs into the passenger seat, and the other into the back, with me (this last one is the one I saw clearly). The one in the back (also a boy) shoves another gun into my ribs and tells me not to look at his face, to look at the floor. I look at the floor, I swear I look at the floor while the man yells at me to tell Julieta to get into the van. "If you don't, dickhead, I'll burn you up, I'll burn you right here." That's the phrase, yes, that's the phrase that still sounds in my ears.

There's a sequence that's difficult to recreate. Me yelling at Julieta to please, get into the van, and simultaneously, Julieta drawing away. They are only fragments, it's worth saying, pieces that I can't tie together. There are many pieces. But there, in the front, is Julieta, Julieta's face, between anguished and firm, Julieta fearing for my life but at the same time understanding that she can't get in, that she can't do anything. Julieta steps back (she's still stepping back: it's an image that won't leave me) in slow motion. She steps back decisively and the man, evaluating the situation, screams again, "I'll burn you, dickhead, if she doesn't get in I'll burn you." Now I don't know in what moment Julieta (Julieta's face) disappeared, stopped reflecting in my window.

We are on the Solano (in my memory we have never left the Solano), we're going down the Solano. The boy who's driving accelerates suddenly and brakes unexpectedly amidst the traffic. The ride is epileptic. The boy asks me if the alarm is activated: I tell him it's not. The boy asks me for the car's registration: I tell him it's in the glove compartment. The boy asks me why Julieta didn't obey me: I tell him that it's better this way, that my wife is very nervous. "Who wears the pants in your house, dickhead?" It's a question that I didn't know how to answer, that I have never known how to answer.

It's useless to proceed: to explain that from the Solano we arrive at Plaza Venezuela, that we then go up the Andres Bello, that we cross the Urdaneta (the fearless police in Miraflores), that we continue to the San Martín, that we cross the bridge at Caño Amarillo ... And there, at that point, suddenly, in the middle of the bridge, they ask me to get out, and I immediately get out. "Fast, dickhead, fast." That order resounds in my ears.

What sense is there in recapitulating all this? I don't know. I can't explain it. It's for the time, I suppose, to understand the measure of time. Time tightens in these situations, it turns to dust. Absolutely, I remember nothing. They were forty minutes of nothingness. I calmed myself, yes, and I tried to relax the three boys who were visibly upset. But I did it in a fog. My memory is like a fog, like a state of unconsciousness.

The ending (if one can speak of an ending) I have recounted to my friends: Five minutes later a police patrol crossing the bridge over Caño Amarillo picked me up. The men took me to the first station they encountered and there they asked me to help them create a spoken portrait. "I don't remember anything," was the first thing I said to the police woman who was drawing. "Well," I corrected myself, "I remember one of the faces, the boy who rode in the back with me, a bare flannel shirt, short hair, curly, cut close to the bone, a dark face, clear, large, the beginnings of a mustache, four pimples on his forehead ..." An order that I altered in each one of the five descriptions that I made, a routine that I repeated to the officer.

The point is that I wanted to see myself from outside. Or, in other words, that I only saw myself from the distance in this story. The one in the car isn't me, I'm not that nocturnal victim, about to be murdered in his own car. The point is to ask oneself how the story flows, how it imposed itself. From the moment when they opened the door, I stopped being me. I saw myself. And that, I think, was the only way I could save myself. Putting myself above the situation, removing myself from the situation. I see the scene, yes, like a little god, like a portable god that saves, splices, refines, feeds the sequences, gives them meaning.

I recompose the boy's face whenever I can. But it's an equivocal, mobile face. It changes whenever I want. It's a spoken portrait, and every description is different, every time I speak the face comes out differently. The narrator has no alternative, the narrator reconstructs the vision as often as he wants (on drives, at parties, having dinner with friends) and the victim—who is also me—suffers, has suffered, still feels the pistol jabbed into the left side of his ribcage.

With a Blind Man's Cane

Everything begins on Armando's eyelid. It's all there. He has been stung on his eyelid, a wasp sting, and the eyelid grows and grows. It swells way up. He has a flap over his eye. Armando sees double or he doesn't see at all.

The wasp forces us to sum everything up, in instants, only in instants. We had recently moved to Santa Sofía and it occurred to us to climb the hill that rose behind the house. And Mama: "Not up the hill; don't go up the hill." And us, secretly, to the hill. A slow, variable hike, a bit dangerous: Armando, me, and a few new friends from the neighborhood.

Deep in the underbrush—dry, spiny, gray—somebody steps on the hive and the wasps came screaming out. We ran the best we could, our behinds sliding along the ground, rolling downhill, raising a cloud of dust. We were a human river descending a forgotten riverbed. And the wasp. of course, the wasp confidently nailing its stinger into Armando's eye; the wasp there, hidden, punctual, as though responding to a plan, to a call to ruin our day. The stinger makes us swallow thick saliva, it decomposes us, it projects us into an unknown territory where we advance throwing slaps in our path.

It's all eyelid, we repeat, a growing red eyelid. A bruise of an eyelid. And us, sure, in the middle of the underbrush, far from home, sneaking out from home.

It was my eyelid (that was how it felt). The eyelid called me. Armando, my little brother, at this stage does nothing but cry and I feel I have to act for that eyelid. Armando cries: not from pain, I think, but from fear. A fear that overwhelms him, that makes him grab hold of everything: he held onto the bushes, he held onto the ground, he held my hands. Pure fear, and pure screaming. A eyelid swelling on those eight little years.

We descended. We had to climb down the hill. The friends, by now, had left, they had disappeared in the retreat. Only me and Armando. Only Armando, me, and the growing eyelid. Our misery was double: the eyelid, of course, but also our explanation to Mother ("Not up the hill").

We arrived home (I was covering Armando's mouth so he wouldn't cry, so he wouldn't scream) and a miracle occurs. I go to the fridge, pull out a lemon and squeeze a dripping line of juice over Armando's eyelid. The eyelid retreats, yes, it begins to retreat. The eyelid is shrinking slowly. A retractile action, a muscle pulling itself in.

Armando returned to life, he returned to the world of the seeing. The eyelid was still red, but in its place, not out of proportion.

After that, we saw the world in a different way: without venom, without a stinger. Maybe Armando doesn't remember it, but that day he learned to see.

Sovereign

Of Irene, only her photo. We see her there, with her face wrinkled up (maybe from the sun), in a grand white dress (pleats and more pleats) that covered her knees and a crown that tipped with every movement of her head. We were at Carnival and Irene was our smiling princess.

The problem was—how can I describe it?—the prince, choosing the prince. Ms. Sanchez, the principal, wandered through all the classrooms without finding a candidate. Lots of beat-up boys could be found in Bachaquero in those days: lots of scars, lots of sweat, the stench of monkeys.

Strictly by elimination, the choice fell on me (I added my wrinkled face to Irene's). There we are, well, the two of us posing for history, two eight-year-old sheep turds, with the whole retinue gathered around us (pages and valets), with confetti and streamers.

In that era, water had not yet dominated the sense of play. We would say that we emphasized that monarchical exercise almost out of longing: the procession lengthened itself, the greetings of the delegations, and Irene and I with wrinkled faces.

The photo allows me to reconstruct the episode and maybe nothing more. The rest (everything that doesn't appear there, something that we could call the future) we don't know, we'll never know.

I wanted to follow Irene's trail, the beautiful sovereign, Irene. The last news, years ago, told me of her graduation as a doctor from the University of Zulia.

That little wrinkled face contained her future, and I imagine that today many of the sick that await her treatments remain captivated by her royal manner.

Chen the Chinawoman

This is my face. I see it often in the mirror, I look at it carefully in the mirror. I am the perfect confluence of my parents. Here all of the features flow out, all of the differences. These eyes, for example, aren't from either one of them, they're from both of them: the blue of the iris I inherited from my mother, but this eyelid gathered at its end is, undoubtedly, an Oriental evocation.

My father is an expert in public policy and my mother specializes in the situation of widows in India. They are both professors at Harvard University and they met there when they were students.

My father, Edward Chen, is an American of Chinese extraction; my mother, Elizabeth Rutherford, is a British subject. I superimpose their faces one upon the other and the operation seems impossible, infinite. My father has features that are definitely Asian (although he doesn't speak Chinese), straight black hair, a short build, slightly arched legs.

My mother is the incarnation of pallor (lots of color in her cheeks), her nose is straight, her body long, her hair blond (a tuft permanently clouds her eyes).

But from those two faces, superimposed, affixed, unique, comes mine. I have a bit of everything; I have them both. From my mother, the height, the svelte movements, the blue eyes, the snowy complexion. From my father, the straight hair, long (a black cascade), the prominent cheekbones, the distant Oriental gaze.

My good friends call me Chen the Chinawoman. I study contemporary dance and I also like photography. My body's flexibility, I think, I owe to my father's muscle tissues (my professors constantly talk about my flexible body). This hidden face that has captivated more than one, this perfect fusion, I owe to my mother, it's the regeneration of my mother's bloodless face.

I grow inwards, I look in the mirror and I grow inwards. I like silence, the deep and vertical space of silence, and I understand now why you too have remained silent looking at my photograph, a stone that falls slowly in the water.

River of Blood

Things don't seem to have names in Canaima. This river, that lake that it forms, the waterfall over there ... nothing has a specific name. That's the jungle, the nameless jungle: everything stops making sense, we lose our senses in it.

The voyage was Uncle Delio's idea (and we'll have to thank him for it for the rest of our lives). A simple idea: to spend three days, a long weekend, at the vacation camp in Canaima. Something planned and well-organized, with necklaces made from seeds, captive monkeys and excursions. Three days of glory, it must be added, three days during which all of the cousins (Ana, Carlos, Arturo, Germán and me) lose our names.

We are already in the airplane on our way to paradise and the pilot announces the imminent appearance of Salto Ángel on our left side. We see it, between the clouds we see it. The image appeared and then it was erased (like in a dream). An intermittent image, a decoy that indicated that we both were and were not in reality. Salto Ángel was offered to us in pieces: the thread of its beginnings, the body that widens, the ancient reddish stretch of ground, the vapor at the end of the fall (another cloud for our dream). And suddenly, following another turn of the airplane, this time complete, the frank, lofty, prehistoric nudity of the waterfall. Something in us understood completely that we had entered another world and that the infinity there below embraced us as its newest creatures.

We arrive in Canaima with the cadence of the waterfall, submerged in the amazement of the falls. The camp was predictable: Indians with necklaces by the landing strip (a hateful degrading vision, "Welcome to Canaima"), cabins planted all along the length of the hill (should that settlement really be called a hill, that urbanizing exercise in the middle of the jungle?), a central bungalow that served as a dining room, the thunder of the waterfall in the background, and, below, the lake before our eyes, fickle as a revelation, placid and at the same time deceptive, with hidden currents that had carried more than one off to the nameless jungle.

The first thing was the color of the water: that specific black that degraded between our hands to red, to brown, to mustard, to the color of urine. A unique, unforgettable color, the color of worn-out rock; a profound breath, full of hidden, secret hues, we supposed. We submerged in that water like sponges, trying to take with us some of the pigments of the riverbed, hoping that our pores would open slowly like carnivorous plants and cease to be pores (lose the name), would turn into something else. Hours in the water, like tadpoles, like tired and happy batracia, but also like dolphins, yes, fresh-water dolphins leaping among the splendor of forms.

The lake had the shape of a question mark and we swam in the superior curve. We were a question in the midst of the jungle, an impulse, a pretext. The water spun around dead trees that displayed their floating trunks like skeletons. They were vestiges of a spent life, of a false resistance: washed trees like floating buoys, like planks of a lost dock that now served only to divide the current. From the beginning we supposed that we couldn't enter the deeper waters: if we barely lost our footing the current dragged at us decisively. We also played with this fear: trying to arrive at that point of equilibrium where the current would just begin to carry us off ...

The second day's journey had also been announced. You arrived at the edge of the cascade, and carefully, along a narrow path, passed behind the curtain of water, reaching some shallow caverns that the erosion of the waterfall had gradually formed over the centuries. It was a vertigo, one more step towards an absolute deviation. We remained there for hours, squatting, sitting as best we could, watching and listening to the uproar. You couldn't talk; the sound of the water was omnipresent. We just looked at each other and smiled, accomplices. Germán improvised a rod and extended its point towards the falling water. In milliseconds the current tore it from his hands and pulverized it. We had death before us: robust, whole, noisy and constant. And we confronted it, we said to it in our language of those days, "You stay over there, and we'll stay over here."

The noise of the waterfall could become a kind of silence, it was so constant. It was a noise without any overtones, affixed to nothing, infinitely continuous. It was also the silence of death, we thought, a quiet silence which let you hear distant complaints, suffering souls. Upon returning, like a reflection that continues vibrating in the retina, the noise continued in us. It was a buzzing in our ears. The sonorous thread accompanied us throughout the rest of the day, reminding us of something, prefiguring something. That night in the safety of the cabin, it was inevitable that we would fall into telling ghost stories. I recreated exactly, credibly, a scene in Lagunillas. I had risen from bed to go get a glass of water, I had put my little feet on the floor, I had seen the frank, callused hand, with knuckles, that held my ankle so I wouldn't leave. Ever since then I have known that someone sleeps under my bed: it's an alter ego, it's my counterpart, it's the creature I saw today in the waterfall.

The third day's journey was the definitive one. We have never been the same since. The jungle suspended us, it made us float, it made us small, it turned us insignificant, particles of a totality, it thought we were lianas, serpents, beasts, drifting spirits. We had to go back up the river that plunges into the falls. We went along one of the banks, upriver, to embark in a dugout canoe with an outboard motor. A short, strong Indian, with a pink shirt, was the guide. He barely spoke: he got by with single syllables and stiff gestures. He suddenly raised his arm and pointed things out: a *tepuy*, an island in the middle of the river, a lateral waterfall. We gradually fell into that compact, summarized marvel that was made for us, lukewarm urban animals. We gradually fell into that vague, steamy enchantment, that hid the names of things from us.

Climbing back up the current of the river meant losing ourselves, entering into the search for origins. The river became narrower with every advance. The only thing that stood out on the horizon was Auyantepuy, the guide told us, the back flank of Auyantepuy: a solid wall of stone (brown, gray, black, reddish) that raised itself like a column of air in the midst of the jungle, an abrupt movement, willful, of wanting to cut the horizon, to impose a limit on the horizon. A sun on the earth. It was our only point of orientation, our only referent.

The guide draws near to the beach on the left side and decides to take a brief rest. The place offers us a rapid, linear, bubbly cascade that rushes over three successive levels of stone slabs to gather itself below in a deep basin enclosed by stones. It was the day's party. The slabs were natural toboggans across which we slid drunkenly until we landed with the full weight of our bodies in the basin ... An instantaneous, cautious diversion, that re-concentrated us in our fears: an appetizer that the jungle offered us, so we would gradually gain confidence in these unknown forms.

We left behind the cascade and renewed the trajectory. The river continued to draw itself into a narrow trench and the black of its waters made it even more closed. A quartz mirror, we think, an impenetrable mirror. Suddenly, majestic and serene, a water snake crosses the river. The guide raises his arm and signals over there, in front. We see a proud head, rising up out of the water, and, behind it, as though it was disturbing the surface, the successive waves of the reptile. We didn't want to imagine the size (it's a conjecture we have kept for the speculation of our days, every time the cousins get together), but in our retelling we have always seen her large, enormous, knotting one bank to the other. We have dreamed with the image of that head in the middle of the river. An isolated image, splendid, momentary, that summarizes the trajectory like a fixed idea.

We arrived at the promised island, the end of our journey. The guide had reserved for that point the preparation of lunch. It was, in effect, an island, a kind of curb that bifurcated the current. A point of the island received us, barely a sandy bank, where the vegetation left a brief clearing. It was a shelter (another shelter) for our fears, it was a perfect space. There we were, marauding, confiscating every piece of the little island, recognizing it: two tall stones, the yellow sand under the water, another basin further over there in the form of a water jug, a prosperous, exciting vegetation, that grew inwards, there where the island opened up.

Germán and I separated from the others, we gradually surrendered, as though we were submerging ourselves in a strange, definitive game, while the guide improvised a fireplace to roast an impaled fish. It was like an abduction. The beginnings were a blessing: low vegetation; dispersed stands of straw, growing, among fallen trunks; bushes the size of a person that projected inflamed shadows. It was our deviation, our placid drifting. We began to distinguish three levels in the vegetation: a highest level, of centenarian trees that captured the sunlight and whose crowns projected a first layer of shadow; a second intermediate level of middle-sized bushes, two or three yards high, that grew at the expense of the protection of the first trees; and a third level, trailing, more ours, where a varied and vital vegetation evolved with total liberty.

At some point, everything became vegetation. We couldn't see the sky: only the protective crowns of the tallest

trees. The light entered in beams through the free spaces
that the foliage granted, tubular tunnels banished the shadows. The island invited and we drew away from the shore.
At first it was a game of swords: two poles that Germán had
improvised with his knife, a precarious type of fencing that
we elaborated believing we were two musketeers of the jungle.
But from this skirmish we passed on to another, a secret
expedition to rescue a damsel in the middle of the forest.
The jungle invited us initially with visible trails that facili-
tated our progress. We spread our legs to jump over the fallen
trunks or some indescribable bush until, bit by bit, without
us noticing, we were in the heart of the great trees and now
various hanging vines were combing our hair.

It was the central moment, the moment of our loss, of
not continuing on, of realizing that we had left behind every
trace, of feeling that we were two more creatures of the noisy
world. The jungle breathed, it throbbed. Its heart must be
somewhere, a red inferno, a great underground bonfire, crackling underneath our feet. We stopped, we detained ourselves
in the middle of nowhere, in the middle of everywhere. We
sat down on a thick, fallen trunk, the bundle of roots hover-
ing ten feet above our heads, with chunks of earth still hanging on it like balloons of suspended water. We sweated profusely and our breath was a presentiment. We didn't do anything: just wait, observe. Truly, we weren't scared. It was just
the merest respite, we said, a brief rest that would permit us
to resume our enterprise: saving the damsel who was captive
in the hands of some spirit of the jungle.

It was hard to believe that we were in the middle of an
island. I didn't perceive the slightest whisper of running wa-

ter. Only the murmur of the creatures, of all the creatures, their panting respiration. A precise spluttering, like the crackling of broken leaves, on the middle horizon of our ears. We heard ourselves: the crackling of our hearts, a small heart in the middle of the immensity, a hot, lurching drumbeat, galloping through the veins that irrigated our bodies, the blood calling to other blood, the blood wanting to rejoin a greater flow, open, totalizing, rivers converging toward a great matrix of sensibility, the bloody origin of the waters. We were a capillary vessel, an artery, a pipe in that great circulation of blood to which all of our liquids contribute: the dry saliva on our palates, the sticky sweat of our foreheads, the urine held in our bladders. Suddenly, as though he were responding to the call, Germán opened his fly and aimed a stream at the base of the fallen trunk: the yellowish flow detached bits of rotten wood, swelling the anthill's hole, creating momentary floods for minuscule, invisible creatures, fermenting the ground, fertilizing the ground, rejoining the secret circulation of the ground.

A rigid hand took hold of my shoulder. It was the pink-shirted guide, by now tired of searching for us. We returned to the shore along a different trail to later encounter the other cousins and Uncle Delio. In the midst of the fish and cassava we found it difficult to explain what we had felt. It wasn't the damsel (we never found her), it was the unnamable wandering off. No. It was something more, something indefinable that we still talk about without respite. It was a perdition without limits: the jungle astray in us and us astray in the jungle.

With time, I have wanted to feel in the guide's rigid

hand on my shoulder the same intensity of the callused hand that held my ankle in Lagunillas. It's the same hand that holds me back, it's the same being. I know that a secret, hidden jungle breathes under my bed.

$\mathcal{M}igrations$

No invention is greater than the duck, that counterpoint fusing all of nature's variables. A perfect organism, a mechanism. Feet to swim, wings to fly, a beak to pick grain. And we aren't speaking of more exotic examples: we pass over the sublime swan (a duck which unequivocally repudiates the water) until we examine a variant only seen once in Bergamo, Italy, a species of hen with red eyebrows extending in a construction of cartilage whose glare doesn't stop assaulting us for hours. All this variety, I repeat, concentrated in only one species.

I want to see the ten-year-old boy again, the boy who cultivated his favorite variant in The Hague: a compact organism, with black feathers and an iridescent green plume, that splashed water without getting wet, and hurried across the pond without any great commotion. Good swimmers, better walkers and scouts of the skies, those ducks accumulated in the winter and they scattered in the summer.

The boy went religiously, every winter afternoon, to see them at a canal near his house. Watching the animals swimming in the middle of the frozen waters and shaking off the snowflakes that fell endlessly, was an outstanding show.

The impression I retain is that the boy was also a duck. I don't know how to explain it. Every game, every prank, revived the versatility of the ducks. He emulated those low flights, grazing over things, the flapping of wings, the shaking off. I saw him swim in that frigid water, with his iridescent green plume, splashing among the floating chunks of ice that spring had already broken loose.

It was his answer to the climate, to adversity.

Ducks have got nothing to lose, thinks that boy today as he walks through any city. His persistence—invariable—gradually projects them in any reservoir, in any hidden bit of water, in any public fountain. He sees them, he imagines them, and by now that exercise is like having a good omen for the weather.

The boy doesn't have a history and, unequivocally, it doesn't matter. He has ducks, he has the authority of the ducks, he has the key to migrate through the skies.

Now hidden, now lacking a voice, the boy—who is no other than me—seeks to return to that unequivocal, liberating quack-quack.

The Replica

I have just finished poisoning Victoria. Her body lies there, quiet, stretched out over the bed, one arm raised with the palm open over the glass top of the night stand, a thread of brandy sliding from the right corner of her mouth. I don't see her eyes, they're turned inwards. I'm still sitting in her living room. It's night and I don't know why I write these lines. I look towards the avenue, towards the lamp, towards the objects, trying to clarify things for myself. But it's useless. I know that I should call the police, I know that I shouldn't delay.

I was born in San Lorenzo, in the state of Zulia, exactly thirty years ago. My father was an oil worker; my mother, the cook in a restaurant in Ciudad Ojeda. They raised us moving from place to place all along the eastern coast of the lake. Tamare, Tía Juana, Cabimas, La Salina, Lagunillas ... for me each of those names evokes specific circumstances and precise images. My home was humble, beyond a doubt. But over those simple, precarious forms, my father always made an effort to plot a scheme, an order whose inspiration escaped him, a design which obeyed hidden impulses but which he always tried to orchestrate rigidly. His manners were like a husk of sensibility. He chided our table manners, without knowing if the correction was accurate; he slapped us every time a swear word escaped our mouths; he tore up our dresses if by chance the fringe of the skirt raised above our knees. He could never see us in sandals or slippers, never. It was an impulse; it was like operating from a vacuum.

My father threw all of his effort into our education. The four children (two boys and two girls) had to diligently bring home good grades. My father oversaw every assignment, he attended all of the school ceremonies, he personally picked up the monthly report cards, he conversed with the teachers and professors, he cheered at all of the school games. His salary disappeared searching for the best schools in the region, paying high monthly tuitions, covering the alterations of the uniforms, the equipment, the textbooks.

None of us will forget my father's punishments. A bad report card could mean many things: being shut in your room, being grounded for days, weeks of no chocolate or sweets, whippings with his belt on the legs and, in extreme cases, when an F came in, walking on your knees around the back yard. They are images that we'd like to erase, but they remain there, floating, palpitating. We don't know what strange force led my father to cross over the line. It was a force that dominated him, that overpowered him. My mother watched him practice all of this from the kitchen in silence, without ever intervening, and later, when she could, she would come to our rooms and console us (I see my head resting on her shoulder, I can still see it).

My father whipped my buttocks in the third grade. Since

then, I have cultivated a secret vocation: I think I have been straight, decisive; I think I have applied myself to things, I think I have looked for the meaning of things. My life changed irremediably when I left home. I turned eighteen and they had offered me the opportunity to go study in Maracaibo. My father's sister, my Aunt Celia, would put me up in her small house in Los Haticos.

The university dazzled me. It's hard to describe what it meant to me: all the people, the movement of all the people, the classrooms, the lecture halls, the classes, the libraries, the innumerable disciplines, the professors. Victoria was a classmate in my freshman journalism courses, and from the moment we met, we were intimate friends. It's hard to think of how everything started. I see her face—carefully styled black hair framing that pale face—at the moment when she came over to me to ask for a study guide. Her manner seemed affable, affectionate, and I wanted never to separate myself from her security, her stability.

We spent our college years together, we built our lives together: midterm exams, interminable study sessions, essays, schedules, the best professors, even our free time. I took notes for her when she couldn't come to class or she took notes for me when I woke up feeling sick. A deep emotion grew between me and Victoria; a sisterhood grew, a dark root. Victoria came to know my secrets, the tensions in my family, the men I could have fallen in love with, my hopes and also my hatreds.

Some time passes before I begin to emulate Victoria, time justifies Victoria's ways. It's hard to say when everything began. Maybe with Victoria's hairstyle, with her beauty salon. I wanted to form my hair into those dark, curvilinear, quilted locks, so they would encircle my face. I wanted to transplant Victoria's pallid skin color with baths of cream and powder. I wanted to copy her clothing, the correctness of her style—neither too ostentatious nor too discreet. I gradually modeled myself in her form, and in her manner.

Afterwards it was Victoria's humor, her sharp guffaws, her mischievous winks, her talent for over-acting at key moments (an oral presentation, a job interview), her vocabulary (certain words of hers that I repeated until I made them mine), her gestures, the intonation of her voice (emphasizing what should be emphasized and lowering her tone at the right moment).

Destiny separated us after graduation: Victoria became the principal writer for a magazine dedicated to politics, and I kept an eye on her from a radio station. And I followed Victoria: her texts, her adjectives, the often unruly form of her syntax, the way she structured her articles, her attractive summaries. I copied that style precisely, making it mine through the radio station's news bulletins. In every crime, in every strike in the oil industry, in every oil spill in the lake, Victoria's unmistakable style, now mine, now in my hands.

Victoria received the Municipal Journalism Prize for a very popular series about contraband in La Guajira and her name was discussed in every corner of Maracaibo. I yearned for that distinction for my news dispatches; elegantly written and presented. I called her to congratulate her. I invited her to dinner to celebrate her prize.

I saw her arrive punctually at the restaurant. I brushed her cheek as we hugged. It had been a long time since we'd last seen one another and I admired her face, as always, snowy, serene, encircled by her hairdo. Those forms are mine, I thought, and Victoria stole them from me with mastery, with enviable mastery.

Nothing is very clear. We drank brandy after dinner and we continue drinking in the living room of her house. Victoria tells me about Aníbal, a co-worker whom she is thinking of marrying, two years of loving, plans to move in together.

I have felt many emotions tonight. I have wanted to dispose of Victoria, of Victoria's face, thinking that I could finally recover something of my own. I have wanted Victoria's cadaver, stretched out, a mortal poison mixed into the brandy, to discover myself, to finally accede to myself. I have wanted to be Victoria; now I am Victoria.

But it doesn't matter. I'll get up and I'll call the police. It's me who they must search for; it's my cadaver dissolved on the bed that is awaiting them. Without Victoria I am nobody and now that I am dead my life has no meaning.

—*for Milagros Socorro*

Logs in the Water

We didn't see the dock. I swear we didn't see it. The only thing we remembered was that Susana, Simón and I were water-skiing behind the boat. We had managed to convince Alvaro to take all three of us out on the water with a motor that was barely seventy horsepower. And up to that point everything was great, we were proud of our skill. But then Alvaro goes and complicates things: instead of going toward the Grand Canal, which was what we had in mind, he decides to take a shortcut down Caño Copey and put us to the test.

You can't water-ski in Caño Copey. We knew that. Going through there was more than an adventure; it was a risk. You never knew what you'd run into there (Susana assured us she had seen the red eyes of a crocodile). It was a wild channel, overwhelmed by growth along its flanks, with half-fallen logs in the water. It wasn't easy to navigate. You had to respond to each successive bend as the channel turned this way and that, with a sense of anticipation and true mastery.

Alvaro turns into Caño Copey and we're behind him, the three of us behind him, stunned, unable to believe what

Alvaro is doing: Susana was in the middle, Simón on the left, and me on the right. From behind, at the time, we scream at Alvaro, "No, don't turn in there." But Alvaro didn't pay attention to any of it. Alvaro laughed, yeah, Alvaro laughed at us, seeing us behind the boat, pulled along by the boat, crossing Caño Copey.

From the moment he confronted the channel, Alvaro stopped seeing us. He was concentrating on his maneuvers, on the unexpected turns, on the sand bars. Letting go of the line and abandoning the ride became an impossible reaction. We were scared of sinking in that water and we knew that Alvaro was playing at not turning around under any circumstances. On top of it all, we thought, it's not one water-skier, but three. So we maintained our spaces (on the turns, for example, when we went to the right, Simón closed in and I had to open up). Poor Susana, trembling on her little feet, stayed in the middle and tried not to cross over into either of the other two wakes.

We came along behind, concentrating, careful, feeling that we floated over a forbidden path, that falling in those waters could have meant anything (a baba, an underwater net, some channel monster, the Creature from the Black Lagoon) ... We came along behind, ignoring the clay of the riverbed, a pasty substance that Susana had once grazed (layers of leaves, earth, dead animals) ... The water in the channel seemed stagnant and Alvaro broke that black mirror with a wake that shocked the peacefulness of the banks and made the mangroves along the shore reel.

Nobody wanted to fall down, nobody could fall down. Susana, the least expert in these affairs, was rigid on her two skis. She didn't look to either side (we helped her out): she just concentrated on what Alvaro was discovering out there in front. Susana anticipated Alvaro's maneuvers. If a turn announced itself, she tilted herself in time; if a log along the edge obliged us to pull in tight, she was already pulling in before we came upon it.

We couldn't believe it: we were coming out of Caño Copey. You could already see some of the houses in Cangrejal. Alvaro leaves the channel and enters the principal canal of Cangrejal planning to continue on into the Grand Canal. We couldn't believe it: to be leaving Caño Copey, to have successfully crossed Caño Copey, three at once, upon the water. The tension reduced itself; our muscles relaxed.

We are in Cangrejal's principal canal and we abandon ourselves to that symmetry of the banks: the low walls of the houses, the open gardens, three royal palms standing together, the beating of the water against the boats tied up at their docks. And Alvaro begins to look back, and Alvaro begins to celebrate the crossing of Caño Copey, and Alvaro begins to laugh, to make fun of us. Alvaro with his hands on the steering wheel twisted backwards, making gestures with his hands held up, sure of his prowess. Alvaro who lets the boat drift towards the left bank of the canal, slowly.

We didn't see the dock. We didn't see it and we came on it and hit it directly. Alvaro hit it with a powerful impact, he broke it in two, a thunder grew from logs scattering all across the water, the shell of the bow broke loose, we discovered it later. And us, pulled along behind, we turned into toys: Simón, on the left, got caught up in the initial row of logs that still remained standing; Susana, terrified, crossed her skis and tried to sink in the water to keep from falling flat against the motor's propeller; and I, opening out to the right, got stuck suddenly in a sandbar.

A man with a broom came out of the house by the dock. He screamed and threatened to drive us away. Later we found out that his name was Capodiferro: for weeks he pestered Alvaro's father, until he had charged him the last possible cent for the damages. The man screamed from the shore upon seeing his dock torn to bits, dissolved in the water.

Alvaro didn't react: the nape of his neck was hurt and he massaged it unconsciously with his right hand. The impact had surprised him completely and the strain on his body had pulled all of his muscles. The boat was in the middle of the canal: the accident had thrown the stick shift into neutral and the propeller, spinning out of control, threw off a flood of bubbles without advancing at all. Alvaro began to loosen the cords and one by one he pulled us into the boat. We left Capodiferro screaming from the bank in an image that reminded us of a cartoon.

We ended up in Río Chico Hospital. We exhausted (also) Alvaro's father's patience. Simón came out with bandages on his arms (he'd had to use them as a shield against a log that was coming towards him), Susana with bruises on her legs and me with a strange pain in my back.

I carry the boat accident on Río Chico like a stitch. And every time I twist in a certain manner my back reminds me of it.

Paper Boat

I was kissing Sonia along the way. I was kissing her gently along the way. They were just barely caresses of my mouth, like the brushing of birds across a lake. Everything seemed to be yielding. I thought no, not with Sonia, I thought nothing would happen. But it occurs to me to take her hand, I don't know why I think of holding her hand, just like that, holding it and caressing it, and I see that Sonia also opens her hand, and I feel that she responds to the caress. And I can't believe it, Sonia there with me, in the car, responding, relaxing. And then, of course, I stop the car, I search for a place to park. I was giving her a ride to her house, there, in Altamira, I was bringing her home from school, I had been bringing her since the beginning of the school year, always taking her to her house, every afternoon. And Sonia, of course, how can I tell you, Sonia's beauty, Sonia's face, something like a paralysis, like a rapture, like an abyss. We are riding along in my little car, calm, and then, around the area of the Country Club, laughing at something, I think yes, I see her face and I think, yes, I should take her hand (for months I've been thinking of taking her hand), and I see that yes, a caress, yes, that everything responds and I start crying, I swear that I start crying with Sonia, in my little car, caressing me.

I had to stop the car. I couldn't go on in the car like that. I looked for a small, quiet street. And the kiss, I begin to kiss her. First her cheek, yes, then I eat her lips, I suck her lips. That red meatiness of Sonia, a mollusk, a firm fiber that I still feel between my teeth. And afterwards, Sonia's tongue, Sonia's hot tongue, a long serpentine thing, a viper that submerged itself firmly, that explored the walls of my mouth, that recognized each of my teeth. And then there, in the hidden street, everything is slow, everything is placid. I, truly, would die with Sonia there, all of Sonia mine there. And then my hand over her chest, slowly my hand over her breast. I knew that she wasn't wearing a bra, since that morning I had known, and I pass my hand over her shirt and I feel a firm, attentive, reserved fruit, a muscle, yes, another meaty fiber. And I put my hand in her shirt, I slide it in this way, and Sonia moans, pants, a captive, thirsty animal. And that image of her legs, the color, yes, of her legs, a late suntan, opening itself under her skirt. Like a compulsive movement, scissors that cut, a beautiful, eternal, contained spasm, and my other hand, also slowly, barely traversing the softness of those thighs, the infinite smoothness of those thighs.

Drops fall on the car. Scattered raindrops. A diagram of water on the windshield while Sonia again submerges her tongue in my mouth. I like the rain, I felt protected by the rain. My little car is a cabin and I'm with her in the cabin. I think I imagine fog over some lake and me in a cabin by the lake with Sonia. We didn't want to rush. Everything was slow: her mouth, her right breast, her left thigh. Everything felt slow, interminable. We didn't know where we'd end up, we didn't want to know where we were going to end up. And Sonia's saliva that floods my mouth while the drops evolve into heavier drops and now they're darts against the car. Sonia slowly over me and the rain there outside. A breeze that transforms into a wind, imaginary mist that turns into real fog, and me and Sonia in our cabin.

It rains cats and dogs. And Sonia and I separate to look at the rain, to see ourselves beneath the rain. I remember that we looked in each other's faces and we were kind of embarrassed, to discover ourselves there beneath the rain, kissing beneath the rain. I see Sonia's face in the car. I see her face leaning back in the car and one of her hands, gone astray, that caresses the nape of my neck while her eyes explore out beyond the windshield. The rain that covers us, the rain that buries us. Now they're arrows, a wet hail that drums against the shell of the car. The little car submerged beneath the rain and the visibility reduced to zero. Everything fogs up in the car and we are turned into water, the water of our bodies breathing the only hot air that resists under the rain. I remember that we stayed like that, our mouths separated, watching the rain that enclosed us. We were scared, sure, for a moment, we were scared, wondering at the force of the water that was falling. We heard a gushing underneath the car and it was the current rising over the street. A river that carried earth, branches, rocks; a current that dragged everything along. I wanted to believe that the current swept us away, I wanted to believe that it would pull us along, car and all, down the street. The torrent moved us, it shook us, it pushed us with sudden gusts. And me and

Sonia there, detained, breathless, our hands holding on to the straps, our arms tense, our mouths separated, our thighs closed, our bodies incapacitated. And Sonia's beauty, a detained beauty, a wet beauty, all of her wet, wet from sweat, from saliva, wet from breath, from oxygen that we exhausted in the cabin of the car. Sonia's face, unforgettable, unearned, all of Sonia there with me, the rain, the rain that dragged us.

It cleared up. It cleared up suddenly, too. We didn't know what to do. We didn't know how to restart anything. I turned the car on and I drove Sonia to her house. Upon arriving, she said good-bye to me with a kiss, wet, on my cheek.

The Pain

Upon reading this letter I want you to forget about me, I want you to think of me no more. I have been nobody in your life: only your shadow. I have thought I was keeping you company, but in reality—think about it carefully—you have always been alone.

We gradually constructed this scene, this slow scene. I still see myself with the first day's rose: the rose of the first date in the first restaurant on the first night. I also see myself among the sheets of the little hotel in Macuto where we made love three days in a row. We didn't leave that little hotel in Macuto, we were incapable of leaving.

I thought that you loved me, I always believed it. I thought that the scratching of your chin across my belly was the sign of love. I believed in your kisses, I believed in your hands, your lukewarm hands taking mine. I believed in our children, in our beautiful children.

I think I have nourished the scene: the ferns around the house, the Sunday breakfasts, the paintings that we bought together, the great double bed that we installed in the master bedroom.

I have slept with you every night of the last ten years. I know your breathing, the trembling of your breathing. I know the tear that descends from your eyelid in the early morning. I know the thread of saliva that escapes the corner of your mouth. I know your smells. I also know your dreams (that recurrent ostrich that pulls his head out of a hole to show you that his eyes are plastic). I know the moles on your back (I guarantee you I've counted them). I know your body, the shape of your body, the muscle full of blood that sinks straight into my center.

I have been here and it's as if I had never been here at all. I can't manage to understand it. All of this has been mine, strictly mine. I have nourished the meaning of things. We have constructed a home, our home, with furniture, flowers, meals, friends, children and us, us together in our room.

I have thought I had you, I have thought I had you at my side. It's a sensation that doesn't desert me: that of your company. Being with you. Seeing life with you. Suffering with you (one suffers less, I believe, when the suffering is shared). Your face is mine, your thoughts are mine. That's what I have always believed, that's what I have always felt.

But everything has changed. I don't know when it started, but everything has changed. I only remember one scene, one recent scene. We're naked, in our bedroom, making love, and suddenly you pick me up and you carry me to the balcony, and there, standing up, you take me, passionately, me leaning against the glass of the balcony and you behind me panting. I felt your rhythmic pushing and saw the city. You projected me against the city. I came happily, I swear that I came happily and I loved you deeply in that moment. I can believe that I was happy there, intensely happy. I was with you, yes, but the pain also made me feel lonely, profoundly lonely, like I had never felt before. It was a distance, it was an irremediable outcry.

And now I discover (or I have understood through intuition): we can never be with anybody. No matter how much we try, we can never be with anybody. Our acts are attempts, it's practicing at company, at a complicity. We love, yes, we scratch and scrape, but they are like sparkles of the impossibility of being together. I can't penetrate you nor you me. I put my head next to yours in the moment of greatest communion, when your flesh is inside me, and I feel that your head continues to be yours, distant, inaccessible. Love, I repeat, is a pantomime, it's the façade of an impossibility.

That's why I'm going away, that's why I'm leaving you. I believe I love you, I believe I will always love you. But love is insufficient, it's a limited sense. Then I would prefer to live deeply this condition of ours going from body to body, knowing that I will also never know the others no matter how much I agitate their bodies. In the background, maybe just barely, we can only search for ourselves, discover ourselves. And that meeting, it must be added, is also severely painful.

I thank you for everything, truly. Our shared life, this tentative construction, our children, our spaces.

You'll find this letter next the keys to the front door. Take charge, please, of everything and try to explain to our children.

I beg you never to search for me. You won't be able to find me. Imagine that the one who was with you never ex-

isted. In truth, you were always with yourself. I was only the
pretext for you to meet yourself.

— *for Yolanda Pantin*

Oxygen

It was like an intoxication: Bernardo talking incessantly during the whole trip. He didn't stop for even a moment: he was a little parrot amidst fog and *frailejones*. And there was one recurrent, obsessive theme: thieves. Thieves in all their permutations: with and without swords, with and without revolvers, masked or without masks, alone or in groups, thousands or solitary. In Bernardo's mind, God did battle with all evil beings, no matter how great their number, and triumphed. "God against a thousand thieves," he repeated, "God against the bad guys, God against all the devils."

We thought that the landscape would capture him, would suspend his discourse. And, certainly, it did. We knew that the fog, the light rain, the cold of the high plateau, were ideal for mystery, for some horror story, for ghosts. But from there to jump back to the singular subject of thieves was a great distance.

The route was attractive: a few pine trees, *frailejones* everywhere in all of their forms and sizes, moss stuck to the rocks, the little river that you crossed putting your feet on four rocky crags, a horse or two that passed by.

We were going to Black Lake from Mucubají. It was the day's appointment, the day's challenge. And maybe the deeper motivation was to see Bernardo in the scene. And, of course, we saw him in the scene. Just as the route began to turn down the hillside, Bernardo detached a dry stalk from a *frailejon* flower and improvised a sword. From there on, it was all thieves.

We guess that it was the oxygen, the lack of oxygen, that turned him monothematic.

Since then, every time we climb to a peak that approaches twelve thousand feet, a Bernardo of exhaustive and eloquent spirit imposes a new theme on us.

Reversible

Marie-Ange has never existed. Her face never existed, the black rimmel of her also-black eyes never overflowed, she wasn't short. We never met in a hallway of the University of Paris and I never knew that she was divorced and had a lively ten-year-old son.

Her car wasn't a Renault. You didn't catch the train to go to her house at the Gare Saint-Lazare. Her apartment wasn't on a second floor and her bedroom never overlooked an interior courtyard full of flowers.

Her bed never was a hard mattress thrown on the floor. Her window never shook with the blizzards and the rain.

I didn't sample her body. I never extended myself over that pale, anxious surface, that didn't await me every Friday night and that didn't not give up until dawn.

I never went to a Genesis concert with her son; we never got excited listening to a Phil Collins drum solo.

Marie-Ange didn't exist. What exists is the incisive memory and I'm the only one who insists on making it flesh and blood.

Speech

I don't know my father. The last time I saw him I was four years old. I remember only fragments of his face: maybe the color of his hair, his smile, his red eyes.

In the last scene that I remember he's hitting my mother. My mother flees those blows, runs to my bed and wakes me up. My mother puts me in the middle, my mother uses me as a shield and, seeing me, my father stops for a moment.

Since then, day after day, I reconstruct his image. I have imagined him in every manner: tall, fat, skinny, loving, harsh. At Christmas I always see him arriving with gifts under his arm.

I have dreamed of my father. In my dreams he has been a prince, a bully, a king, a dragon. He has been a jungle, too, once he was a jungle full of thorns. In all of the dreams I am always asleep and, while I sleep, I dream that he comes to wake me up.

This exercise is the real substance of my days. I live among images, and at the end my father always appears to stay forever.

I want to ask him, wherever he may be, to come to me,

to come to me now and acknowledge me. I will always receive him, day or night, live or dead, prosperous or unfortu-
nate. I want to tell him that I'm his daughter. I want him to
know that if his leaving was because I was once used as my
mother's shield, he can come back and beat me, too.

Madrigal

Juan Andrés broke his femur before he'd turned one. I am rocking him gently in a swing, and I see how the protective wooden bar, rotted by the rain, splinters. I tried to reach him as he fell but I only managed to stretch out his leg and intercept him half way with my thigh. The doctor says that the fracture was produced there, when he hit my leg, and not when he hit the ground.

The X-rays were funny: you could see the broken femur, like the A-frame roof of a house. A bony knot began to grow there, a bump that was covering the fracture.

We had to set a cast around his whole little waist. It was like a plaster loincloth. The boy crawled with difficulty, dragging his cast. Not to mention when he had to make peepee or poopoo. We had to stick big balls of cotton between the cast and his skin and pull out the waste. It wasn't easy. The cast began to stink and we daubed it with alcohol and cologne.

After a month, we took the cast off. The boy walked all arched, but bit by bit he straightened himself out.

Now he's a complete, straight young man, but I can tell

you he doesn't like sports much. He's an indoor child, who reads a lot and has only a few friends.

I still have the X-ray of the fracture. I look at it on the light table and I tend to believe that re-grown bony knot carries the exact memory of the fall.

Pitched Battle

The Venezuelans' version:

The tree had always been ours. It was a big, leafy rubber tree, with thousands of branches, that had grown in the vacant lot behind Mrs. Blanca Baralt's house. We slowly accommodated the tree. We built an enormous house, almost a fort, with broad planks. We had bedrooms, meeting rooms, a kitchen and even a bathroom. All of us who lived in the country met there, always. We practically lived there. If we didn't turn up all day, our mothers knew where to look for us. Also, it was one of the few places in the area that was truly free and open. There weren't any wells or fences around it. It was an esplanade of dry, dusty terrain with trimmed weeds. We arrived down any one of the streets and from any angle, the tree opened up our vision; it was an enormous, imposing thing, our habitual den. We planned everything there.

The Dutch version:

The tree was empty, abandoned. There were a few old splintered planks. Thomas was the first to climb up and he encountered a filthy mess: open cans, cardboard boxes, papers, dry leaves, bird shit, milk cartons. It was disgusting. We cleaned out the house: we swept, collected the trash, added new wood, brought fabric to make curtains, found some metal screening to keep out the mosquitoes, and we bought a gas stove. We liked spying from the tree. We could see everything from the windows. It was like being elevated above everything else. We formed a club, a fraternity. We were an organization: we had rules and established habits.

Daniel Quintero's version:

I went by there at about four in the afternoon. I was going to the club's theater and I took a shortcut through Mrs. Blanca's backyard. I saw that the tree was occupied by the Dutch kids and I didn't understand. A few looked at me through some little holes as though they were spying on me. I didn't say a word: I pretended not to understand. Then I ran to the club and told the others. We didn't stay to see the movie. We went to the tree: we went to combat. We were all there. Upon arriving we stopped about thirty yards away, practically at the edge of the block. A delegation (composed of me and two others) went to speak with the Dutch kids. We were walking towards the tree when we saw Thomas climb down (he lived next door to me). We explained to Thomas that they had to leave, that the tree was ours, that they should please just come down. He said no, that the tree had been abandoned, that they had fixed it up with new wood, that they were staying there.

Thomas Volkenborg's version:

I saw Daniel and two other boys approaching the tree. I know Daniel because he lives next door to my house. I climbed down from the tree to talk with them (I'm the only member of the group who speaks Spanish). Daniel told me that we had to go, the tree was theirs. I told him no, that the tree had been completely abandoned, that we had cleaned it and fixed it up, that we were staying, that they had no right to any claims on the tree.

Security Chief Juan Camacho's version:

We received a call from Blanca Baralt at about five in the afternoon. She complained of noise and gunshots. I myself went to the scene, just in case. When I arrived, I didn't understand anything. There was a cloud of dust hanging around the rubber tree. From below, a swarm of boys were throwing rocks wildly. From above they were also throwing things. I heard something that sounded like gunshots, it's true, but I couldn't understand where they were coming from. We had to intervene. It meant we had to throw ourselves into the melee of dust and rocks. We put on our security helmets. We had to calm down the boys who were throwing stones from under the tree: they were unrecognizable, flushed, frothing at the mouths. A few cried from fury, others punched the air and indignantly gestured at the tree. We pushed all of them into one of the vans. I had to send three of my men up the tree. They managed to remove roughly fifteen children, all sons of the Dutch. We sent these into one of the other vans. We had to take a few of them to the clinic. At first we didn't notice, but there were various injured among the group. It was all very confusing.

Mrs. Blanca Baralt's version:

They were all crazy: the Venezuelans and the Dutch. I didn't understand anything. I was hanging laundry on the clothesline in my backyard and I began to hear shots. I tried to see what was happening around the tree. It was all a ball of dust. Among the clouds of dust I managed to see some children throwing stones and others sitting up in the tree also throwing things. I was scared. I had never seen anything like this. I immediately called security.

Daniel Quintero's second version:

I walked away from the tree and went to talk with the group. I told them what Thomas had said, that they weren't going to leave the tree. We agreed that this was unacceptable, that the Dutch kids were looking for trouble. I returned to the tree: I yelled up to Thomas that they had fifteen minutes to leave, that it was an ultimatum. I said it very clearly. He laughed from the tree, he said that nobody was going to get them out of that tree. Fifteen minutes later we surrounded the tree. We began to scream at them to come down and the Dutch kids didn't react at all. First were the branches, some branches that we threw upwards as a warning. But later it was rocks, rocks against the planks of the tree house. The impact of the rocks against the planks made a sharp, loud noise. We didn't want to hurt anybody: just scare them a little bit so they'd come down. And that's when we heard the first shot and we ran. We didn't know where it came from, but we imagined it must be from the tree. We ran in every direction, we dispersed. It was then that we picked up the glass, chunks of broken glass that were lying around on the ground. We threw them as hard as we could so that they'd reach the tree house.

Thomas Volkenborg's second version:
We didn't understand why the Venezuelans came with this story of an ultimatum. The tree was ours, it was our hideout. We had put a lot of effort into fixing it up, into making the house pretty. We didn't pay any attention to the branches they threw up at us. But then we began to hear rocks. The rocks boomed against the planks. It seemed like a blizzard of rocks. That's when we got scared. One of the rocks hit my brother in the face. A bloody bruise grew on his forehead, it swelled up. We only had the BB rifles. The rock was a direct insult and we didn't have any other way to defend ourselves. First we shot up in the air, to scare them away. But then, when we saw that mixed in with the rocks they were also throwing glass, we began aiming at their legs. We were terrified that a piece of glass would reach us. We were very scared.

Fatboy Sánchez's version:
I felt something like a needle in my leg, something like a dart. The pain made me fall to my knees. I didn't know what was happening to me. I searched my right leg and I saw a red spot on my pants, getting bigger. I realized that I was wounded. I got very scared. I shouted. I yelled for the others to help me. I was unprotected. I was afraid that someone else would hit me.

The younger of the Van Dallen boys' version:

I heard a buzzing and I saw that something had cut my abdomen. My hands went to my stomach instinctively. I bled, I bled profusely. It was a piece of glass, the round bottom of a bottle. I saw the blood amplified by the bottle and I got scared. I fainted when I saw that my friends were coming to help.

Alfonso Costa, the doctor in the clinic's version:

The wounds weren't very serious. A lot of bruises and cuts. Only three cases required special treatment: the head wound from a stone suffered by the younger of the Volkenborg boys, Dr. Sánchez's son's BB wound, and the glass encrusted in the stomach of the younger of the Van Dallen boys. In the first case I applied compresses and disinfectants; in the second case the BB was extracted, it was almost superficial. The one who suffered the most was the younger of the Van Dallen boys; we had to keep him in the clinic three days. He had to receive twelve stitches. The wound was wide: the glass opened an extended aperture below the bellybutton.

Thomas's father, Mr. Volkenborg's version:

We bought the BB guns to hunt iguanas. The iguanas run up onto the roof of the house and they don't let us sleep at night.

The Statue

This is my belly. I hold it with both hands as I look in the mirror. I like being naked in front of the mirror: it's a unique, intimate, pure sensation. My belly has something of a bulge to it. It's a dark-skinned belly, round like a light bulb. I see my nudity and I think I understand that it's mine, all mine. But this nudity was also Julio's. Julio perused it as he wished, in every possible way and at every possible hour. His tongue, for example, was here, above my belly button. His hands kneaded this light bulb of a belly, his mouth sucked these breasts. I don't know why I remember everything under a bloody moon.

We met in Paris. By that time Julio was a well-known sculptor. I went to one of his exhibitions in a small gallery on the *rue du Dragón* with a Venezuelan friend. From the moment we were introduced he didn't stop looking at me. He conversed with someone else and he was glancing at me out of the corner of his eye, he toasted with a tall glass of champagne and he looked at me, he spoke with the gallery owner and he looked at me, he explained something to a collector who was interested in a small piece and he looked at me. That same evening we went to his studio and we stayed up all night. I entered already admired into that high-ceilinged space, with pulleys and chains that hung from rails, and my high heels kicked up dust. There were newspapers and buckets of water all over; there were neon pieces; there were bottles of brushes, spatulas, tools; there was a compressor to spray films of paint; there were cork panels with clippings and reproductions of Giacommetti, Picasso, Rembrandt, Botero, Moore. And a little higher up, at one end, was his room. His room was like a terrace peeking out from the heights of the studio. A little corner with an ample mattress, two night tables and a little refrigerator.

Julio concentrated on my body all night long. He didn't give me a rest (he didn't give this belly a break). He traversed this body like nobody before: he kneaded it, probed it, massaged it, caught it in his arms, lifted it up, wet it, penetrated it for moments, let himself come out again to start all over. It was like that all night. I remember a yellow light (a bloody moon) that protected us in the room. An indirect light, like a flame, that illuminated our bodies. We saw only what we had to see. Everything was almost in darkness. We couldn't see our faces; we could only guess at them. Julio divined my face, my body, my hands, the form of my belly.

I was happy with Julio. Why should I hide it? Julio turned me into the center of his days. Everything was done together: the walks, the trips to the country, shopping, the cafés, the lectures, the concerts. He didn't give me a respite. He always appeared in my little apartment with a red rose (I changed the water in my vase every day). Little by little, without my noticing or giving it much importance, I began to stay over in his studio every night. We began to live together; we grew into a routine that we loved. We returned to Venezuela for a month just to get married. My parents didn't understand that marriage very much, but neither did they oppose it: Julio began to appear in the art sections of our newspapers.

We returned to Paris and continued to cultivate our habits. Julio cooked, organized parties, invited friends, coordinated dances, and, most important, worked in his studio like a possessed man. I would awake with my eyes still half-sticky and look down from the veranda of the bedroom: Julio would be there, immovable, pulling the cord of a pulley, carrying a pail from one side to the other, mixing clay, hitting a piece of marble with a chisel, drawing sketches on the light table. It was a spectacle to see him work with that passion. I admired him and, from that distance, I loved him. And he, rhythmically, at night, continued to investigate my body with the zeal of a watchtower guard. I did almost nothing, I abandoned myself, I let myself be traversed by that constant creativity that didn't give me a rest or a break.

There was a moment of crisis, of getting lost in himself. Julio spoke very little. The meetings, the walks and the daytrips all stopped. I saw him meditate for days in his studio without finding a specific direction. One night, weakened by the attack of his mouth, his arms, his manners, he asked me to come down to the studio and sit naked on a stool. I saw him evolve before my eyes, also naked, feverish, with substances and stones. He looked at my belly, fixedly, he crashed against my body, and his hands convulsed over the clay or struck the marble with precise hits. There were successive nights of kidnapping; I, worn out, half-asleep, posed for him.

I didn't understand what was coming out of it. They were bits, fragments, unfinished plots, angles of the body. Julio grouped the pieces together and he exhibited them in the gallery on the rue du Dragón. "A Reading of Magda," was the title of the exhibition, and I recognized bits of myself in that collection of objects. The exhibition was a public and critical success. Julio seemed to be reaching a climax, and a prominent critic from *Le Monde* published a review called "The Signs of Maturity." The exhibition traveled to Berlin, Milan, Venice, and finally, to Warsaw.

It never should have gone to Warsaw. It's a point on the itinerary that only brought me pain. Julio wasn't the same when he returned from Warsaw. Something had happened in Poland and I discovered it bit by bit. Trips to Poland, stays in Poland, supposed interviews in Poland. And finally, a woman in Poland, a poster designer with whom he fell madly in love.

I left Julio, I left the studio, I left our routines. And I have missed that whole world immensely. I follow his path in the newspapers and through our common friends, but it has been good for me to be far from him. It has been hard work reconstructing my life. I have realized that Julio penetrated me intimately and deeply. I have had friends, but no lasting relations. At the moment of truth, when another evolves over my body under a bloody moon, something stops me in bed. A strange sensation: it's as if they were watching me, it's as if this stomach belonged to Julio, as if this little belly that I'm looking at were his.

I have absolutely been afraid of surrendering myself to another. Or more accurately: I don't know how to surrender myself to another. It's a skill I have forgotten. There is something that I reserve of my intimacy: a belonging, a piece of a body, a fragment of skin, that's not even mine, that still is and will always be Julio's.

The Summit

They say that Santa Ana Mountain was originally an island. The ocean gradually receded over time and it ended up tying the mountain to solid land with a fragile isthmus, covered with sand dunes. Today Santa Ana Mountain crowns the peninsula of Paraguaná like a compulsory reference. You perceive the mountain from all points on the peninsula: nearby or far-off, crisp or hazy, certain or like a mirage in your vision. Its peak rises some twenty-four hundred feet above sea level—short in reality, but it stands out forcibly in the endless flatness of the peninsula.

For the unusual traveler who lives lost in Paraguaná, the mountain doesn't stop being a certainty. It's the only figure that contrasts with the rest of what the peninsula contains: rocky terrain, trees, thistles, cacti, prickly pear and a wind that never stops blowing, that is capable of bending the most robust of trees. The ocean breeze that bathes the peninsula along the eastern shore combs the plant life all along its journey and creates a permanent buzzing in our ears. In Paraguaná, there is no silence. Or, in other words: silence is the background noise of the wind, immutable in our eardrums. You can count the seconds when the wind stops (a hollow, the ocean's losing its breath, an atmospheric depression) and offers an absolute, vacant, original silence. But these, I repeat, are rare moments.

We had been looking at the mountain from all possible angles: from Cape San Roman, from Tiraya, from Adícora, from El Pico, from Cardón, from Amuay. The mountain like an unalterable cipher in the middle of the wind, like a great magnet that we circled everyday, coming and going from one end of the peninsula to the other, without daring to give in. We respected that sudden elevation of land and, above all, we were scared of what we saw on the summit: immense boulders of cut rock that piled together like giant moles (if not like tumors) and ended up deforming the oblique green line of ascent.

We resisted making a journey up the mountain. We stretched out the seven days of the week in the peninsula's other reflections: the salt works, the beaches dotted with fossils and pelican bones, the bays, the dunes, the coral reefs. This secret impulse separated and united us, we reserved exactly the last day to scale the mountain. The group was big: eight children and five adults divided among three families.

We got up early that day (we slept in some cabins in Cardón) and we rode to Moruy in the three vans. From there we began the climb. We went out into the open country, with neither tools nor preparations. We always supposed (at least, that's what they had told us) that the ascent took roughly three hours at a quick pace, and the descent was always easier.

What the mountain felt on its foothills from the beginning was a murmur of voices, a colorful humanity, an absurd invasion. I imagine that remote tickling that the mountain must have felt on its foot, that itching that calls out, and the wise patience in which it must have wrapped itself in order to offer an open door to that retinue.

Along the walk, as might be expected, we gradually drifted apart from one another. We formed three groups: three in the front, four in the middle, and the rest behind, resting on every rock they discovered and intercepting the littlest kids who always get distracted by anything.

The first vision was unforgettable. It was like a measuring of forces, it was like the real encounter with the mountain. The mountain let us know that we were entering foreign territory by showing us its first embassy: an imposing pack of reddish-green locusts that sat quiet and frightening along the edge of the path. The first reaction was to turn back: grab all the kids and return from this foolishness. We feared that the pack would fly up and cover us like a cloud. Captivated by these cartoon figures that carpeted the length of the earth, the children cultivated a silence that emulated the locusts' secret tension. We were still barely in the foothills of the emanation and already this first encounter paralyzed us. We decided to distance ourselves from the main path and follow a rocky trail to try and rejoin the main path further along.

The second vision was no less extreme: Miguelito, Maruja's youngest, wanted to grab a black vine that curled around the base of a prickly pear, and a mapanare snake awoke from its sleep in the shadows and sinuously twisted off among the rocks. Miguelito thought the scene was funny. But we, the adults, had our hearts galloping in our throats for hours. It was another sign that the mountain had sent us and again the idea of turning back crossed our minds.

By this time it was hard to coordinate the group. We were clearly three sub-groups and I went ahead with my daughter Lucía and with Mariana, Maruja's biggest. Lucía and Mariana, both of them ten, proved their agility running over the rocks, and they didn't mind dragging themselves along on their bottoms should the path demand it. I felt comfortable in their company and I understood that the elastic flexibility of their bodies invited me to maintain the pace that continued to separate us more and more from the rest of the group.

We couldn't see any other members of the group when the path led us to the intermediate peak on one of the laterals where for the first time we could see a segment of the peninsula. In the foreground we saw the church in Moruy and its plaza, then an endless strip of land splattered with vegetation, and at the end the refineries of Cardón and Amuay and finally the improbable blue tongue of the ocean. The view was already imposing and a translucent protective blanket lowered from the sky pressing our bodies against the earth.

Towards one side the lateral offered us the peninsula, but towards the other, the one that awaited us, the mountain opened up a dark and impenetrable mouth. It took some effort to understand where we were. The mountain established a clear borderline between the vegetation of its foothills—dry, xerophytic, skeletal—and that of the summit—humid, abundant, overgrown—and we found ourselves just on that fragile frontier. We suddenly understood that the elevation of the terrain went in search of a more humid climate, possibly offered by the low-flying clouds, and a cooler temperature. A new, specific habitat designed its own landscape.

The change was frankly abrupt and unbelievable: multicolored birds, high-peaked trees, vines suspended from inaccessible arbors, clay instead of dry earth in the path, leaves the size of Lucía or Mariana that threw themselves in our way. The buzzing of the wind persisted, but now it was much more humid. It was, if you like, a lighter, more perfumed buzzing. A virgin jungle palpitated beneath our feet and every puddle that we clouded with our steps agitated that open heart, that naked heart.

I should add that Lucía and Mariana began to become bewitched. The sun that had tanned their foreheads during the first stage of the hike had disappeared now to offer them this sinuous, cool, muddy route, along which they threw themselves headlong as if they were searching for a fountain, for a lost spring. They ran like little devils, without worrying about any sudden shock, and I followed their lead with difficulty. Nothing was strange to them. They felt welcome, embraced by that landscape of clay and rocks, and with every step they re-invented the path believing solely in the instinct that led them to choose one trail and reject the others.

I assumed that the others had abandoned the hike. The lookout on the lateral hadn't allowed me to see anybody on the route that snaked up the foothills of the mountain, I understood that I was alone with Lucía and Mariana and that the challenge was now greater, it was strictly ours.

The sun gave us tubular beams of light on the path and,

through the gaps that the crowns of the trees granted us, I could see the closeness of the clouds brushing the summit at great velocity.

Now I must speak of our loss. Because that's what it was about: a serene drunkenness, a deviation where the mountain added us to its whims. One route divided the jungle in two halves and we didn't want to abandon it, no matter how attractive the vegetation that overflowed both flanks might be. At this point, we were different people: our pants were covered with mud from so much dragging and stooping, our arms were covered with dried scabs of clay, Lucía and Mariana's locks dripped like springs over their cheerful faces.

In its latter stages the mountain gave us a high façade of rock that could only be conquered by climbing it upright. A thick vine that swung from a high-up branch was the only sign. Lucía and Mariana climbed the wall, holding onto the vine, and they greeted me from above as if they were challenging me. I had to follow them, but not without losing my footing on more than one occasion. Over the base of the rock ran a creek that all along its route fed a slippery and invisible moss.

Having climbed the wall, we entered the final stage, the third and final stage. We were at the summit, undoubtedly, and the jungle fell back to leave it naked with only rocks planted all along its length and some low bushes, like beach grass, that shook spasmodically to the rhythm of the wind. Here the path sunk into the bed of the rock and the trail also remained bordered by rocks that served as handrails. We advanced slowly along this definitive trail that the landscape cleared for us until we set our feet on the last, thick, smooth rock that allowed us to crown the summit.

What the summit gave us is an unrepeatable exercise, and it's useless to try and condense into a single sequence all of the images that our eyes retained. There was the peninsula in all of its splendor, all of its four coasts: the isthmus to the south, the lighthouse at Cape San Roman to the north, the beaches of Tiraya and Adícora to the east, the two refineries with their great gas flames to the west. There was a tall white cross that some explorer had left in times past. There was the wind, stony, free, omnipresent, with gusts that didn't let us stand up, that obliged us to stoop and hold on to the low rocks; an originating force that dragged everything along in its path; all of the winds of the peninsula gathered together at that point, coinciding in the whirl that lifted us up and suspended us in the air.

It took Lucía and Mariana a few minutes to recognize that the translucent image that brushed the summit with colossal tufts of cotton were the clouds themselves crashing defiantly against the summit. Before the fear of losing their balance due to the ferocious force of the clouds crashing in, before that always-distant presence that suddenly turned material and wrapped them in shaking, Lucía and Mariana didn't know what to do but fall to their knees and understand that only a God could animate the force that vigorously nailed them to the earth.

Trilogy

I have three sons by three different men. The first was a Kurd in the resistance living in exile in Paris; the second was a Belgian from Antwerp, a functionary in his country's embassy; the third was a Chilean painter who had his studio in the Place d'Italie. I had relationships with all three while I was still a young student in France.

I have raised my sons with passion. Since my return to Caracas, my mother has had to make space for me in her house in San Bernardino. The boys run around and play in the garden. They are three brothers with three different last names; there have been certain difficulties when it was time to enroll them in school.

Each one inherited a different trait from his father: the oldest, the green eyes and height of the Kurd; the middle one, the straight hair and the indifference of the Belgian; the third, the distant self-absorption of the Chilean. I like this variety, this symphony. It's like having my past fresh, running around the house; it's like having all the variety concentrated in one place.

Strengths and weaknesses accompany me; also the good

and the bad moments. Some days are happy (the birthdays, the day trips) and others truly wretched (the recurrent nightmares of the littlest one). The boys develop without ghosts and I have tried to make paternity a remote idea compared to my mother's warm home.

I see each one's face and I think I am seeing each of their fathers. They are interwoven sequels: the encounters in the cafés, the parties, the parks, the trips to the movies, the museums. They were distinct worlds: from the lurking danger of the Kurd (a true paranoid who couldn't meet me in a café without constantly looking in every direction), passing through the Belgian's diplomatic coolness, ending in the Chilean's romantic passion, always jumping from his canvases to my body or vice versa. All of that richness runs through me from head to tail and, upon remembering, I tremble, I long for the past.

My sons have grown up without any great traumas and I can say that now they are young men. What a shame that with such a great variety no man wants me now. Occasionally I go out on a date with one or another but I have learned to omit any reference to my sons. Each day the boys spend more time with my mother and less time with me. I know that they'll be fine at home. Taking them anywhere is a problem in the agitated life of these times. I have begun to travel with a few friends, I have met other men. Only this time I have taken care not to leave any traces.

The Runaway

Again the feeling that I'm slipping away, Maria, again that recurrent dream. And it's that I wake up in the middle of the night, and it's as if they've just deposited me in bed. I haven't been there, in bed, I have been on another horizon, in another instance, and to convince me of the contrary they return me to my bed just seconds before I wake up. That's the sensation. Last night, I can assure you, I was scared, deeply scared. It was a central, blind, primal fear. I wanted to just call you in Caracas, I wanted to believe that everything was fine with you and the children. But I chose to calm myself down, let the shock abandon me. And of course, I couldn't go back to sleep. It took a long time for me to get out of bed, I was scared of getting out of bed. Then I traversed the studio like a sleepwalker. I approached the work table and I wrote, *Again the feeling that I'm slipping away*. It was the title of this letter, of this story. I can't let the days continue to pass, I say, without being able to decipher the text of this dream that won't leave me alone.

Don't start thinking that Bellagio has been what I expected, what we saw in the pamphlets. Its beauty is paralyzing, without a doubt, but the bad weather hasn't left us. This is Bellagio in September, they tell me: rains, blizzards, storms over the lake. The Center has put me in one of the studios in the residency and from my window I have a clear view of the lake. I can assure you that I have detailed everything: the reddish and mustard-yellow villas along the banks, the ferryboat crossing from one extreme to another, the villages that grow all along its length; these mountains whose summits undress themselves in craggy rocks; an insomniac, majestic moon, made from yellowish candle sperm, that seems like the drain toward which all the bodies of the celestial vault flow. They are the images from my window. These images have been fragmentary, perceived as if in flashes. Only a week ago an electric storm granted us six straight hours of lightning over the lake. It was a counterpoint of lights: when it wasn't the lake reflecting the rays, it was the gray peaks of the mountains that appeared like ghostly presences. Of course there was an immediate blackout: we had to work with candles in our rooms all night long.

But I return to the sensation, to the sensation that I'm slipping away. Let me try to explain. The week has been mild, if you will. I have tried to fulfill the arrangements of the Center. As always in these cases, there have been delegates from all over the world: some presentations more interesting than others. The Center offers everything so that one can concentrate deeply on the work. Reality is always so dissimilar in these encounters: while the representative of Nigeria speaks of how in his country there are four hundred languages, the Norwegian will softly sing a lullaby of his native folklore. It's the whole universe concentrated in one point, in one place of unforgettable beauty and that universe, exactly yesterday, wore me out, debilitated me. I decided to go up to my room after dinner and review my Silvina Ocampo book. I read a clear story, *"La última tarde,"* and I think I took the images of Porfirio Lasta's, the central character's, dream into my sleep. I slept heavily (some brandy with dinner), and suddenly at three in the morning (I could prove it afterwards with the clock on my bedside table) the sensation that I was slipping away, that they had pulled me out by the roots, that I would never return to this conceived, planned, everyday life. And I try to return to the final images of that dream and I can't find them. I only encounter the images of Porfirio Lasta, that unclear dream in which they come to find him at the ranch and they sink a red-hot brand into his chest. I want to find my dream, my specific dream, and what I receive are lashes, residues of the night. And in that emphasis on unearthing, on rediscovering the images, a central, material fear surges up, paralyzes me, to make me feel that I could have been another. I couldn't fall asleep right away, and all the noises of the night magnified themselves: a cat in heat twisting like a rowdy child, a dog barking (maybe because of the same cat), a movement of boxes that rise and fall (an unclear noise). And I didn't want to get out of bed, I was deeply scared to get out of bed. And I searched for forms in all of the forms: the curtains, the mirror, the little lamp on my night table, the phosphorescence of the clock's hands.

After calming myself, I only hit upon walking around the room, on reacquainting myself with it. I approached the work table and noted *Again the feeling that I'm slipping away,* so that some residue of the night would remain, a reference,

so I wouldn't think that I had dreamed everything. I wanted
to write a story (it was the only manner of scratching at the
dream), and I also wanted to write you this letter so that you
would know the dream doesn't abandon me and that to dream
it again, so far from you, remains fearful to me. In Caracas I
have the certainty of your sleeping body beside mine, I have
the arm that I touch and capture in the middle of the night,
I have your placid face, fertilized with tranquillity. But here
in Bellagio, no, here in Bellagio the dream persecutes me
and I am its prisoner.

I have decided to write the dream. Or more precisely:
decipher the text of the dream. I went back to sleep with this
certainty: I would write a story about the dream, and that's
why I wrote down the title. I tried to string together the story
while I fell back asleep, I tried to weave the sequences while
I listened to the cat in heat. And it wasn't easy: I didn't hear
the dream, my dream. I heard more prosaic things: the beating of my heart cornered between my ear and the pillow, the
bubbling tremor of my intestines (again the residues of the
brandy from dinner or of the dinner itself), the brief whisper
of wind against the curtains. Everything except the dream,
the images of the dream. And it's always that way: I dream
everything but I remember nothing. Dreaming is a territory
which is given to me in the exact instant of its development,
that doesn't reserve any influence for times of sleeplessness.
And I, from my sleeplessness. trying uselessly to catch it,
trying to decipher it. And it's useless: I can't conceive of it. I
only hear the dog, the cat in heat, that strange noise of boxes
of fruit that rise and fall in the early morning in a market not
far away. And I am gradually sinking into sleep (I sink like

Porfirio Lasta's red-hot brand) without any hope. And I don't know where I am going, where this recurrent dream wants to take me. In its arms, abandoned, I will again be the victim of its designs, of its writing, and my other me, he who writes this, won't be able to decipher anything afterwards.

And all that remains is the letter, María, this letter that I write now as I lean over and see the lake before Bellagio. This will be another day's journey, working with the Nigerian and the Norwegian, infinite languages that cross eagerly, precise tower of Babel whose thicket we try to untangle day by day. And I wake up this morning tired, with the hangover of last night. And I remember the blows of the dream and my rude awakening at three in the morning. I don't know if the dream returned to carry me to its origins. At least I don't remember. Only the memory of the sudden awakening, I prove it, gives me some indication. And it's possible that last night's intent has been my last temptation to fish for the dream, to decipher its meaning. I have gotten up, María, and I have wanted to write you this letter (before writing a story about the dream) and, on sitting down at the work table, how can I describe it, I have remained petrified, my blood has frozen all at once. I have encountered my note, yes, the trembling calligraphy of the early morning that says *Again the feeling that I'm slipping away*, but below it, in a corner of the paper, another calligraphy no less trembling that is not mine has noted *But you're not going yet*. And suddenly, from the hollow center of my fear, I have understood that this letter that I am writing you now is also the story, that it can be nothing but the story of the dream.

Occurrences

I.

I try to locate myself in a normal morning: a perplexed fly throwing itself against the glass that separates it from an open space. These scattered readings, this extremely contingent posture, always backed up by a cigarette that burns endlessly, perched on the border of the abyss of an ashtray. I would say that I light only one match per day, I would say that a butt on the point of going out lights the virgin tobacco which offers the next mouthful. Will I be deft at emptying ashtrays, will I be the goldsmith forging this paralysis? The lava, the distant lava of desire, flowing ever so slowly down the fields, adding material to the thirsty soil. These portable eruptions, cultivated by the headboard of my bed, inseminated by these tortuous anxieties of presence. My skin behind a backdrop, my breath in the capsule that doesn't blanket any hope, my pulse collected in the assassin's instantaneous gaze. Everything is rank and social circle, yes, all of us wait serenely around the turn of the corner. The alleys seduce, in darkness they establish the lofty flanks of surprise. To take a step toward the other, to dare to take it and, afterwards, revolver in hand, smile at the victim. To ambush the night stroller in any alley and ask him in a melancholy tone: "Do you remember Ricaurte in San Mateo, perchance you remember?" Faithful to gunpowder, we explode in bits. The step has been taken, yes; the escape route, constructed. Life as displacement, writing as wandering. I activate the trigger in silence, and I exit shot towards the vast geography.

II.

Paris's instantaneous geography; immutable, leaden landscape. These mornings with colds, these preambles with water up your nose. Well, yes, they have told me that my nose is abusive. "Look at the size of those nostrils!" comments a Norwegian friend as she drains her glass of beer, as she smiles, knowing herself to be infinitely beautiful (she has the universe firmly grasped by the tail). And here I am confined, far from Norwegian wood, from some lake I've never seen. A cold that flows into the flu. And there aren't any lemons in the refrigerator, not even a chamomile tea. The premature death of aromas on this unfriendly morning, nasal mourning that ignores a Paris full of water. Because Paris is exactly that: a drowned lung, a convulsive cough, a horizon established by a window. And I go towards the window, towards the Paris constricted by surrounding ivy that ascends from the foundation of the building. And there are trees out beyond my window: enormous umbrellas that cover some distracted pedestrian. The lemon sets itself up as a goal; the lemon invokes, invites a displacement. To leave the hallway of the building feeling dizzy, show signs of weakness in the street itself. I should have stayed in bed, tried to recuperate, abolish this frothy bag of images with an icepick. Bleed the medusa over my disorderly bed. But there are no lemons in the neighborhood, there's no establishment capable of supplying them. Bitter, obtuse, inundable flu. Flu with neither beginning nor end: only a long interim without borders. To ignore you in bed while the morning's class waits, lose myself in bed while I anchor my pseudopodia on the lips of the Norwegian friend. And I turn unnecessarily, unable to conciliate sleep, and I turn over and over to transmute myself into a Norwegian girl, all white skin, all white origin, a smile nourished with the strength of wood, robust pine trees that will grow in some forest.

III.

Lentil soup today at midday. "Lots of iron," my mother said. Sculpted the carrots, present the potatoes, subversive the onions. Boil the water in the big pot. To elapse, to let a process complete itself: lentil soup. Yes, letting there be an act with bubbles, with periodic glances into the pot. The top is lifted to witness the agitation. The day is like a conciliatory pact, like the armistice of the affected parties. On one side, the sovereign lentils; on the other, this late disciple, this rustic gastronome. Participating in the humility of the lentil, in its secret pulse. Every jump, every ascending deployment, is a woven invitation, necessarily subtle. The lentil would say: "This observer with the abusive nose who leans in over the expelled vapor is lucky; lucky to be able to lend his eyes, his voice, the escape valve to this, my premature death."

IV.

Conical afternoon, afternoon that searches its flanks for some needle capable of making it twitch. I see Madame Pailleux, I see her with a smile, with a pointer in her hand. A light tap on the blackboard to show us a figure: we repeat its name in a chorus; another higher up to point out an object: we repeat its name in a chorus. Spanish mother? Madame Pailleux? Yes, a Spanish mother. The Norwegian girl smiles at my side, she sips a bit of coffee. That's why she had so much charm, Madame Pailleux, that's why! Well, yes: we celebrate that Navarrese smile in some stray moment of the day. An ample lip that was born in some gray mountain range, that guards some dentures in the hoary Pyrenées, that agonizes with saliva in a Parisian sneeze.

V.

An appointment with the Norwegian girl in a café in the Cité Universitaire. To drink beer with this abusive nose? Well, yes: to drink beer with a Viking echo ... And alone: maybe I ignore myself in this glance that scrapes you, skin and mouth, maybe I don't see myself in this obsessive enumeration of your presence. Be quiet, Odin's creature, be quiet while you tip the glass. And remember: as long as you close your eyelids, as long as you bring your eyelashes to that abrupt and retractile limit, as long as you dare to do it, there will be some God killing himself.

VI.

Incorrigible night ... this one when I wake up to drink a glass of water. Night without the Norwegian, without the flu, without a jump. Hermetic night, imposed on the fabric of silence that an inalterable rainstorm constructs and reclaims. Here I am with a glass on the edge of the window, here I am suddenly in pajamas, here I am with an animal yawn. I ignore everything at this hour, I ignore everything in this lookout. Drink water for water's sake, moisten a chest that is only found outside, that only inhales the air from outside. Broken fragrance, without origin. A fragrance installed over there where it should be located. Over there where it should remain, there where maybe it'll die under the fast wheels of the first buses. Knowing that there is no presence. Knowing that the night is merely an ascending line, an indeterminate flow, a lazy undertow.

VII.

This route 21, this bus route with old people who claim their seats at every stop. This way of smiling at the driver in the Porte de Gentilly, of knowing that I'll have to get off at Les Écoles. This succession of hands on one of the stainless steel tubes: that girl's dirty fingernails, the protruding veins of that fifty-year-old, the callused palm of some woman from Martinique, that woman's unfriendly knuckles. Maybe a model, maybe she's a lover, maybe she's a panther, yes, maybe wanting to be a panther and nothing else, knuckles that are no longer unfriendly knuckles but claws, precise claws, anxious to weave an ambush for some innocuous hunter. And I draw my gaze away from the succession of hands, from that little community of extended arms when the identities play at ignoring one another. And I draw it away to turn it now outside, some series of trees, the Parisian's geometric flora, always sheltered by previous agreements. Foliage in order? Yes, foliage in order, leaves that autumn calls its own, that fall in search of voracious sewers. Norway has told me that she also takes the number 21 from Cité Universitaire, Norway has told me so. But I have never managed to see her. Resigned, I get off at Les Écoles to encounter her minutes later at the feet of Madame Pailleux, as though her morning bird exercise supported the professor's fragile smile. Pointer in hand, we begin ... I start out being this fruitless desert, this tacit mobilization towards the unexpected, this rambling without a previous fruit. And I confess: I don't need the number 21, this imposed journey, to hide my nomad's condition. I am a nomad under this lamp that blankets me, a nomad before this white page, a nomad for my cough, for my cigarette about to fall into the ashtray, another burn for this precarious work table, another look out the window, the same trees, the same rain, my rain, to be this substance that I see, to be this aquatic scattering, the revolt of the oceans falling in their own origin or discovering suddenly the palm of my hand.

VIII.

I fear that nothing makes sense. I fear that these ascensions don't lead to any goal. I fear that these sudden start-ups of the bus are really imperceptible braking. I also fear that Norway is not the opening into the next act. I definitively fear that there is no creation in all of this, no refuge, no link ... The bird ignores its path from one branch to another but, nevertheless, it lets itself be inhabited by the spark of flight, by the desire that strikes it in mid-flight, that imprints on it the address that was unknown until that moment. I leave the house completely blank, I exit without credentials, without an eye that controls, touch that dictates, without advancing beyond the names of the things. I exit looking for an obstacle, a blunder, a black and blue toenail caught in a closing door.

IX.

I have thought I saw Norway in the opening and closing of the refrigerator, I have thought I saw her climbing the badly lit stairways of her building. There must be a straw welcome mat before her door, there must be an appropriate gesture to her hand after having opened the lock and dead bolt on her door. Norway enters a necessarily carpeted apartment, with pillows scattered around the floor, with a vigorous fern in one of the corners. There could be books in some niche of not-precisely-horizontal shelving, there could be a blue vase bought on a trip to Normandy, a faded tulip. A pan half-filled with milk on one of the electric burners, the remains of an egg in a frying pan. Her elbow tries to get comfortable in the carpet as she leafs through a perfectly predictable magazine. Her chin is there, held in the palm of her hand. She grants time to her yawn, to the unnecessity which raising her hand to her mouth turns out to be. Her legs come and go, they cross over in the air, they make the little chain circling her left ankle ring. From image to image, nothing strings itself together; from photo to photo, nothing takes shape. It's time to turn on the bathtub's faucet, it's time to undress. The water fills the bathtub with foam. And a body submerges its whole long length, and a body leans out its island, careless nipple that swells its flesh as it shivers in the cold.

X.

Does Ricaurte still smile in San Mateo? Does his lower lip maybe twist as, cornered by royalists, he aims his gun at the gunpowder? Does he construct some grimace in the middle of his prowess? To abolish stupidity with one single shot, to grow up hidden away, like the indefinable hub of a diaspora. There is only the act, a simple line, a sober and elegant step. There is an abandonment in every surrender, blindness, a broken bottle. And Ricaurte shoots with the precision of a wasp. Desire remains suspended between the gunpowder and the firearm: there is no target but neither is there an origin, there is no Ricaurte but neither is there an explosion. Only displacement, disposal. The bond between one point and another, between one mouth and another, between one abyss and another. Ricaurte's is a wet gaze, a lonely gaze, lacking nothing. Only a shot: the trip the eye takes around the world.

XI.

The end of Madame Pailleux's course. Tonight we'll have champagne, cheese, sausage. And Madame Pailleux smiles from a suede rocking chair, she will counsel future studies, she will propose future encounters. Norway has brought an apple torte; a honeyed circumference that vanquishes my palate. Norway will go to Trieste: some Italian friend that protects the shores of the Adriatic, under a deceptive but attentive sun. Sufficient light to temper their bellies? Yes, at least several decisive rays and a few complicit tangents. Cornered by the conversation next to some jug with giant handles, Norway arranges the universe with gestures. And she speaks of preferences, of her daily getting off in Les Écoles (never witnessed), of the chosen trajectory (always contingent), of the furtive glances of passersby (potential lovers). Can you weave an original path through the abundant guffaws of German tourists? Well, it seems so: smile at a sad Comte in the Place de la Sorbonne, detail with emphasis the new graffiti that Montaigne exhibits on his now polychromed calves, know that Charlemagne is barely just a decoy on the other side of the river. In Trieste there'll be space to trace perfectly predictable trails, dignified sedentary strolls with Gabriela, the Italian friend, high cheekbones before the misguided breeze, some fur coat in the closet ... A full farewell, with some sort of pastry. Rough good-byes from one and another outside the front door. And Madame Pailleux's face is not there, she has evaporated behind the wood. The guests disappear into the open maw of the subway. Black is the palette of the night, black the voices that still reverberate in the night, black is the path back home, my pulse suspended with every step, a dog that barks, the necessary pedestrian who will cross at the next corner.

XII.

To finish somehow, yes, like a wheat harvester that cuts away the chaff, the future germ. Yes, there must be some way of doing it, of flowering in this cloister. I'd have to encounter Norway on the number 21, see her get off in Les Écoles to follow her closely. And it wouldn't be important to ask her what she could be doing at this hour of the night. Well, no, it would be irrelevant. The obvious is that she advances, she loses herself among the guffaws of the Germans. Now she has left Comte behind, and Montaigne too. She's losing herself in the reduced labyrinth of the Latin Quarter, among Greek restaurants and French fries, among clouds of smoke and anxious men. Charlemagne waits on the other side of the river, Charlemagne waits cared for by two vassals. There's a bench that is auspicious for reading, Norway, there's another green bench that could serve as your seat, that could grant a use to the book you stuck in your bag. Let me follow your trail, Norway. And don't be scared: just think that it's a day of classes like any other day, think that for the first time we've gotten on the same number 21. Madame Pailleux's lips are absent, her pointer is absent. Cross the river, yes, towards the bench that awaits you, towards Charlemagne. You'll have to get scared under this streetlight, Norway, you'll have to do it because you don't conceive of such a drifting off. And I follow you cautiously, yes, and I tie you to these lines, to these brusque passages through the Latin Quarter where there aren't only German tourists but also someone following you, who lets himself be carried along by the chain around your ankle, who lets himself be dragged along by that galloping vision. Run, yes, flee among the crowds, take the first alternate route. Run now, yes, towards the river, any street, any alley. And there's a street that opens before your eyes: "*Rue du Chat qui Pêche*," prays the sign. A badly lit little street, a clumsy and rushed choice. I make you grow out from the background of this page, Norway, I make you grow, while you remain cornered. You'll have to turn around now, you'll have to negotiate with the unknown pursuer. And a first laugh blooms, and a first gesture of condescension finds its way. Do you breathe easier before the surprise of a classmate, stammer some phrase? I swell my body up under this lamp, to have the audacity to look out the window one more time, to be capable of ambushing you in this alley, of showing you this steel object with a stench of gunpowder, to ask you in a melancholy tone as I aim at your stomach: "Do you remember Ricaurte in San Mateo, perchance you remember?"

— for Juan Calzadilla Arreaza

II.

FUTURES
AND OTHER TIMES

August 14, 2116

The astronomer Duncan Stell announces in Sydney, Australia, that an asteroid four miles in diameter is blindly flying
through space on a collision course with the Earth. Ice and
rock are concentrated in the meteorite, without the fire of
the trail altering its silhouette. "It will collide frontally with
us, and it will plunge the world into disaster," Stell advises
before an international audience of astrophysicists. "All forms
of life will disappear following an explosion equal to a thousand atomic bombs," exclaims the Australian, his eyes looking out from under his glasses.

The 14th of August of the year 2116, examining the sky
between the branches of a samán tree planted in the middle
of the Barinas plains, my great-grandson Bernardo becomes
aware that another moon occupies the firmament—this one
fiery and omnipresent—and that in a "Hail Mary" the sense
of being could return to the point from which it never should
have emigrated.

The Lookout

The Californian Kip Thorne, attached to one of Mount Palomar's telescopes for nearly a decade, has discovered that the radio-galaxy M-87 is devouring itself through a black hole. An immeasurable abduction throws the peace of the spheres off center and consumes everything that draws near to that sewer-like spot. Thorne writes in a notebook: The hunger of the hole is satiated with one star per year—or its equivalent in gas and cosmic dust.

Return to the Future

Matthew Newman sweats in his synthetic space suit. In honor of the goddess of love, the Greeks baptized with the name Venus this planet whose surface temperature melts lead. Spiny craters and boiling clouds that fly over the poles harry the view of the pioneers. Years ago a mission injected bacteria in the clouds and cultivated blue-green algae in the attempt to create a more benevolent atmosphere. Newman distracts himself with the dust that his boots kick up and, faithful to the new mission, he runs across the first bunch of algae knocked about by the wind. He drops to his knees in a clumsy astronaut's motion and, with his hand amplified by the visor, pulls out that vegetal simulacrum—not without first trembling before an image that has crossed his mind: Venus could be the future of the Earth, he thinks, the last phase of what in the twentieth century they called "the Greenhouse Effect."

November 27, 1992

Blurred by the cloud of images that will spin through his mind just before his death, my son Bernardo will retain the sudden race down the length of the hall of a house in El Marqués: the noise of a bomb that left splinters of bone encrusted in the walls and shattered the glass of a window, reached him in the fullness of his three years between his anguished mother's arms and his absent father's long-distance call.

Our Violent Earth

Tsunamis are common in the Pacific Ocean. Earthquakes of great intensity dislocate the underwater plateau and create a sudden shock wave: the waves are born deep in the ocean and they travel towards shallower waters, growing all along the way. With fifteen-minute intervals and a separation of two hundred and twenty kilometers between them, the waves reach the coast at a speed of eight hundred kilometers per hour.

They tell of forty fishermen in Sokcho, on the eastern coast of Japan, who in 1993 saw a ten-story building of water crashing over them.

There has never been a greater mirror in the ocean than these assassin waves.

Black Palate

Douglas Lin, an astronomer in Santa Cruz, California, affirms before an auditorium that an extreme arm of our Milky Way—a 120-light-year-wide spiral that with celestial generosity pulls along our planet Earth—is devouring a well-known neighboring galaxy called "the Great Magellanic Cloud." A vast halo of dark material invisible to telescopes and probably formed of collapsed stars and exotic atomic particles chokes down its black palate the surrounding cloudiness. Like someone who embraces the infinite with a single gesture, Lin opens his arms all at once and exclaims: "What we are witnessing, ladies and gentlemen, is galactic cannibalism in action."

Rebirth

The Gulf of San Jorge, in southern Argentina, preserves in its bed the dispersed rocks of an asteroid.

Two hundred and fifty million years ago, Tierra del Fuego was broken to bits and an ancient super-continent known as Gondwanaland sent its parts drifting towards what would later become America, Africa, Antarctica and Australia.

It is estimated that ninety-six percent of the species of that time disappeared under the intense disturbance of the impact, giving rise to new life forms.

Notes for a Theory of Creation

All of the universe's radiant energy was liberated during the year following the first explosion, or the Big Bang.

* * *

All matter was grouped together in a single point before being exploded and sending cosmic particles in all directions.

* * *

The fact that thermal radiation is the same in all directions of the universe demonstrates that everything issues from the same source.

* * *

Certain exotic elemental particles must have liberated more energy than others during that first year, shaping the heterogeneity that could have created the gravitational grouping of matter into the formation of galaxies.

Orbital Mirrors

Two Russian cosmonauts, Gennadi Manakov and Alexander Polischok, board the *Soyuz TM-32* spaceship heading for the Mir space station. They know that during operations lasting a full year they will unfurl three "flags," fine plastic sheets forty meters in diameter, which to the common observer will resemble stars in the firmament. They will collect solar light with the goal of voluntarily and unidirectionally projecting it toward any point on the planet.

Three scenes can be enumerated on the Earth during that year: that of a Norwegian fisherman seeing through the smoky window of his cabin how his dark wintry day is turned into a sudden frolic of reflections, that of an agricultural community in Vietnam observing the accelerated growth of the rice they have planted, and that of the rescue teams in Mexico painfully discovering the maximum possible number of cadavers buried under the loosened walls of a nocturnal earthquake.

Dark Matter

Notations of Bernard Saudolet, astrophysicist at the University of California, Berkeley:

Through the centuries we have felt confused by what we see—and also by what we don't see—in the firmament. The serene movement of the galaxies demonstrates to us that there must be at least ten times more matter in the universe than what we can observe. Whatever this vapor that floats in outer space might be, we know that it doesn't emit light or any electromagnetic radiation. Lacking a better name, it is convenient for us to call it "dark matter." The more we advance in our studies, the more we are obliged to recognize that the dark matter dominates and directs the evolution of the universe.

* * *

There are numerous theories regarding dark matter. Some think that it is no more than dust, planets, dead stars, or intergalactic gas. Others propose that the majority of it is composed of strange particles as yet undetected. What we do know is that we need sufficient mass in the Universe to reach an equilibrium between infinite expansion and final collapse. If the mass we see is insufficient to explain how the galaxies have evolved so rapidly, it can be supposed that the invisible presence of dark matter determines the equilibrium of the Universe.

* * *

If we follow one of the suppositions, it's possible that the dark matter is composed largely of ubiquitous particles. If this is the case, we could confirm that thousands of them pass through us every second.

* * *

Despite our belief that we advance in our knowledge and certainty, we always return to the starting point: we only understand one tenth of that which happens in the Universe.

Shark Theory

Annually, in the whole world, only fifty people are attacked. An insignificant figure when compared to the two hundred who, in the United States alone, die every year from wasp and bee stings.

* * *

Of three hundred and fifty species that inhabit the oceans, only twenty represent any threat at all.

* * *

Gastric analysis of examples trapped in fishermen's nets shows that they feed on seals, walruses, dolphins, turtles, octopi, squid, lobster and small fish.

* * *

The reflection of a diving suit, the agitated swimmer on the surface of the water who can seem like a fish in agony, or the explorer who enters his hunting grounds, can be the prelude to a generally mortal bite. Nevertheless, human flesh is disagreeable to the palate of the species. Thus every mouthful is once again expelled.

* * *

It took four hundred million years to see him crown the food chain of the oceans, and only ten for man to assure his rapid extinction.

* * *

The Far East has imposed on our palates the tasty "Shark Fin Soup." The technique used by the fishermen consists of trapping an individual, cutting off his fins, and then letting him go free. Since he can't maintain himself afloat, the shark dies.

* * *

Two-thirds of his brain are dedicated to the sense of smell.

* * *

His vision recognizes certain colors. The retina possesses an ocular element that permits him to reflect images and augment his visual power.

* * *

Certain sensors in his skin, located on both flanks, permit him to read low-frequency vibrations and differentiate prey.

* * *

Bladders located in the snout perceive the bioelectric changes radiated by other marine species. These electroreceptors permit him to hear the heartbeat of any species, even those buried under the sand.

* * *

He is gifted with an advanced immunological system. Scientists recently inoculated one with a dose of cholera bacteria capable of killing twelve horses, and another with a high concentration of carcinogenic substances. The first individual did not manifest any reaction whatsoever; the second did not develop any tumor.

The Last Window

Excerpts from the flight logbook of astrophysicist David Blair, captain of the Voyager XXX mission, partially transmitted to the Earth by the ship's central computer, minutes before impact with a celestial body interrupted communication with the mission.

Gravity's waves have been described as the sky's drums. Minute oscillations in the warp and weft of space pierce all bodies and, nevertheless, are undetectable. How can you calculate this enormous quantity of energy that flows through the universe? That is what the scientists of my crew have been trying to figure out for the last five years.

* * *

Space is the most rigid thing in the universe. It is millions of times more rigid than diamond, the hardest material that we have discovered. Despite this, every time two stars crash into each other or a supernova appears, the fluctuations of the explosion travel through space's three dimensions like a stone provoking waves in a pond. The totality of space is to the ocean what these tiny waves are to a tanker on the high seas.

* * *

Our central experiment has consisted of exposing a two-ton bar of niobium to temperatures three hundred degrees below zero. The superconductive properties of niobium, capable of vibrating for weeks from the most imperceptible caress, will permit us to measure gravitational waves with a fair amount of accuracy.

* * *

Gravitational waves from the original explosion, the Big Bang, must yet be resounding in the structure of space like murmurs in a conch shell. If we can obtain the expansion velocity of these waves, we could lean out that last window and recreate the image of the moment of the Creation, fifteen billion years ago.

The Great Attractor

Scientists have confirmed that the Milky Way is moving at a velocity of approximately six hundred kilometers per second in the direction of the constellation Virgo. The nature of the force exercising this astral inertia is unknown. It is estimated that its focal point must be three hundred million light years away and that it must possess a mass a hundred thousand times greater than the Milky Way, a galaxy that itself contains a hundred billion stars. "If we are correct," says Joel Primack, astrophysicist at the University of California, "the consequences of this pull will be dramatic." The postulated mass of gravitational attraction has been baptized the "Great Attractor."

Apocalypse Now

2000: The median world temperature rises one degree. Inhabitants of Los Angeles and Mexico City use gas masks. Droughts in Africa create hordes of refugees. The borders on the southern edge of Europe and between the United States and Mexico become militarized. Tropical storms take lives in Bangladesh, Australia, and the Caribbean nations. Increasing ultraviolet radiation damages the crops in the Nordic latitudes.

2010: The median world temperature rises one degree. The median sea level rises a foot and a half. Heat waves in Siberia and Canada. The production of grain in the United States, India, China, Russia and the Ukraine reach their lowest levels. The rising sea level contaminates the water supply of the coastal cities. Acid rain and deforestation in Southeast Asia. The demographic explosion and the reduction in arable land create social problems in Latin America.

2020: The median world temperature rises two and a half degrees. River systems of the United States and Russia begin to dry up. The grave droughts in Africa, India and China create a chronic shortage of water and food. Measures of "depopulation" are taken in the large urban centers. The remaining poor people in the city opt for "civic trouble-making." In Africa the UN decrees the first totally depopulated zone on the planet.

2030: The median sea level rises two feet. The construction of dikes begins around all of the world's coastal cities. The influx of salt water into the sewers of the coastal cities causes epidemics of cholera and typhoid fever. Grain production increases in northern Canada and Siberia. The Arctic zones are free of ice throughout the year. Canada militarizes its border with the United States to put a brake on illegal immigration. Marine phytoplankton dies in great proportions under constant exposure to ultraviolet rays.

2040: The median sea level rises three and a half feet. There are millions of displaced people in all of the coastal zones. Twenty percent of Bangladesh's territory is under water. The Nile delta is flooded. Southern Florida is abandoned to the ocean.

2050: The median world temperature rises four degrees. The only grain producers are Canada and Siberia. All of the coastal cities that didn't construct effective dikes are abandoned to the ocean. Tropical wood becomes one of the most expensive materials on the planet.

III.

EXTREMES

The Back Page

We are informed that relatives of Maria Lucena—a native of Córdoba, thirty-one years of age, who battled fruitlessly with a cerebral hemorrhage two hours before her son was born—have decided to donate the dead woman's lungs to a twenty-nine-year-old woman in Almería who suffers from a spontaneous emphysema that has reached its final stage.

The donor died on a Wednesday night without being able to recognize her son—two months premature, three pounds four ounces—who, under strict pediatric care, is in stable condition, victim of severe translucency.

The relatives explain that her other organs were transferred to various centers: the kidneys to Málaga, the heart to Madrid, and the liver to the Reina Sofía Hospital in Córdoba, her native city.

News Dispatch

On television:

9:00 A.M. The newscaster identifies the leader of the rebels. He calls himself Commandant Cat and demands a meeting with the attorney general.

9:02 A.M. The newscaster reads a cable from the France Press agency: "Commandant Cat confirms that the rebellion has been a success. He corroborates the support of the Fifth of July, Third Way, and Red Flag factions as well as the aid of an international neo-Bolshevik section and the socialized Zamorists."

9:05 A.M. The President of the Congress appears. He speaks of the value of the institutions and the salvation of democracy.

9:08 A.M. Commandant Cat again demands the presence of the Attorney General.

9:13 A.M. They attack El Cuño. Loyal officials solicit reinforcements.

9:19 A.M. The Attorney General finally speaks. He says that his office has been addressing the situation for half an hour.

10:00 A.M. Airplanes fire on Miraflores, the presidential palace. Hundred of people, in the renovated O'Leary Plaza, applaud the shooting. *Ole!* they exclaim, every time an airplane approaches the ground.

In O'Leary Plaza:

Two women converse amidst the tumult: the first says: "What's all the cheering for, there are only three little planes attacking?" "Venezuela only has six planes," answers the other. "Three are with the government and three are with the revolution."

Bolivariana, Wire. Stop.

Esteemed President of the Republic: In my files rest categorical answers of ex-presidents ratifying under their administrations the non-authorization of casinos on Margarita. State Governor calls surprise press conference in official residence announcing first results favor installing casinos, primarily to attract tourists. What brings glory to Margarita and fatherland not grottos of corruption but constant and exemplary work in science and literature. Just as we condemn energetically—for duty and justice—repudiated casinos we applaud patriotically Coche head start center dear First Lady's project and beautiful sports complex constructed National Racetrack. His message abounds in projects and ideas deserving study to satisfy Venezuelan patriotism and its antithesis invasion of dazzling crowded gambling establishments doesn't deserve such prize. He who joins integrity as a father, husband, and magistrate, proven cultural passion and perseverance in his work, will control breeze bringing glory to his heart Monsignor Navarro ...

The Executioner's Garden

My name is Saed Al-Sayyaf and I am Saudi Arabia's official executioner. My name is contradictory: Saed means "happy" and Al-Sayyaf "executioner with a sword."

It's very easy to decapitate a delinquent: you only have to separate the head from the trunk. To mutilate the hands, however, I arm myself with more courage: I know that I am cutting off part of a body that will survive. With hands one must always be very sure that the sword will not deviate from its precise course.

I was a farmer until I was twenty and then I enlisted in the Army. Every Friday, after the prayer meetings, I watched how the executioners decapitated criminals in public. I performed my first execution when I was twenty-three: I decapitated three assassins and I earned fifteen hundred riyals.

I have always tried to find opportunities to cut off more heads than hands. It's always much easier and more lucrative. Before separating a head, I lightly cut the victim's shirt in the area behind the neck: I need to have a precise idea of where to direct the sword. Then one single thrust of the sword will be sufficient to make the head jump onto the mound of sand. When it's a woman, I exchange my sword for a pistol; the rules of the Koran forbid the viewing of a woman's flesh.

A recent decree permits the victims to cover their eyes with a black band. Two years ago, the head of a convict I decapitated rolled to a halt at the feet of another who was waiting in line: he died on the spot from a heart attack.

I have been married twenty-four times and I'm the father of twenty-five children. Lately I have been training my son Mohammed to be my successor. I haven't let him practice with a real head but I know that he will do well in the trade.

Now that I am sixty years old, I can admit that, after a time, the job becomes routine: I have cut off the heads of six hundred criminals and the hands of another sixty thieves.

Frequently, before the executions, I stay up all night: the image of the sword not being true along the line of the neck keeps me awake. But I have never had regrets regarding my victims. Once everything is over, I feel satisfied: I have put an end to a life dedicated to outwitting God's laws.

— *for Blanca, again*
(to share in the garden)

Relations

On the second of April, 1976, Graciela Rutilo, nineteen years old, born in Peru to an Argentine citizen of Spanish origin, was kidnapped in Oruro, Bolivia, together with her husband and her nine-month-old daughter, Carla. The Bolivian police turned the couple over to their Argentine colleagues, being sure that the husband had been murdered soon after the border exchange. Carla was granted refuge in an orphanage in La Paz.

On the 25th of August, 1976, the little girl disappears from the Bolivian orphanage, only to reappear a few days later in a prison camp in the city of Buenos Aires where Lieutenant Eduardo Ruffo hid "the disappeared" and where the girl's mother was surely tortured and left for dead.

In 1977, Ruffo, whose wife was sterile, legally adopts Carla under the name Amanda Ruffo.

In 1987, Graciela's mother, exiled in Spain, returns to Buenos Aires with her most precious possession: a footprint of her granddaughter, taken at birth. After this legal testimony, a federal judge orders the restitution of Carla's identity and that she be turned over to her mother's mother.

The press has respected the instructions of the judge and the psychiatrists and has left alone a ten-year-old girl who has to learn to understand that her father was, presumably, her parents' murderer.

Susana's Letter

Eduardo got married last week and, how can I explain it, the pain it has caused me is unlike anything I have known. I have continued the rhythm of my normal life, with good projects: I haven't cried or anything like that. The pain is one of those deep deposits, now ingrained in me. I think it's a pain that will always accompany me, that will never abandon me, even though I follow my normal path. I have drawn and read a lot, and nevertheless, the thought of Eduardo and his matrimony spin continually in my mind. It's a strange sensation. I always felt intuitively that one day this would happen. I feel the loss of something that was already lost for a long time, of something that it was necessary to lose. And it's like discovering the distance before one's eyes, the tip of the needle that wounds you. And, a strange thing, it pleases me to know it so well. For once you know things deeply, from top to bottom.

And it's not the memory of Eduardo. It would be a lie to say that "the memory of Eduardo will always be with me," no, because I don't remember him specifically. It's something else that I carry with me: a sensation, an almost complete life, a shadow, a presence, all broken, but not Eduardo. It's not the man who's studying Engineering, now married to Liliana, who lives in Las Mercedes and who used to pick me up in a blue Renault. No, that's not what I remember. It's not any action, it's not any deed (except one), it's not his body. No, it's something else: It's something absolutely intangible that is within me, it's pure pain, without shape, without anxiety, it's not even called Eduardo, but it issues from him and me, together, not in the past, but in a presence that turns atemporal, that can't be drawn in an image.

Olsen's Island

The Norwegian Fred Olsen is an institution on the Canary island of La Gomera, of which he owns nearly a sixth of the surface. He's a chief, a benefactor, or both at once, depending on who judges him. His family name has formed part of the island for almost a century. His father, Thomas Olsen, owner of the Olsen Shipping Company, knew of La Gomera's existence because it figured in the commercial routes of a few of his boats. He liked it and he acquired land for banana plantations. Later on his son associated with Heliodoro Rodríguez, a local plantation owner, until he fell into financial ruin. Olsen took advantage of the situation and acquired a great plantation in Playa Santiago, at a bargain-basement price, with a hunting range included, where he has recently constructed the only private luxury hotel on the island, near where they are planning to locate the future airport.

La Gomera—an unexploited four-hundred-kilometer ecological jewel—posseses a devilish geography. Its volcanic origin (the sand on its beaches is black) has configured it as a disorderly succession of mountains, nooks, and ravines, to such an extent that the farmers have had to construct four terraces to obtain one that was arable, and they have learned to communicate using a traditional whistle that can be heard from miles away.

In these conditions they have grown corn, plantains, potatoes, and tomatoes some years. Shepherding, fishing and hunting have been their principal means of subsistence—in such an abundance that a third of the population had to emigrate to Venezuela, Cuba, and Tenerife itself.

War Games

The French Navy announces from its general headquarters in Île-Longue that the nuclear submarine *l'Inflexible* will start operations within six weeks.

Originally launched into the water in 1982, *l'Inflexible* was subject to a total remodeling over several months which will bring it up to date with five other nuclear submarines in the fleet: *le Redoutable, le Terrible, le Faudroyant, l'Indomitable* and *le Tonnant,* all in service since 1971 and all carriers of M-20 missiles, capable of generating a thermonuclear explosion equivalent to fifty times the force of the bomb dropped on Hiroshima.

Different from its predecessors in many aspects, *l'Inflexible* will carry a new missile, the M-4, furnished with six thermonuclear warheads and capable of reaching targets more than three thousand miles away.

Due to its ninety-six explosive charges, much lighter and boasting a miniaturized design, *l'Inflexible* alone will surpass the total destructive capacity of the five previous submarines.

Liverpool Heights

A and B are, respectively, ten and eleven years old. One ordinary afternoon they wander aimlessly through a mall located in the outskirts of Liverpool and they encounter little James, three years old, licking an ice cream cone.

James, confident, joins in their complicity: he celebrates their pranks and he lets himself be led by the hand toward a nearby hill where his mother can no longer see him.

Two days later James's cadaver is found half-naked and almost unrecognizable after having been, at the very least, cut in half by a train. The autopsy determines that he was beaten to death over an extended period.

A and B were detained four days later. A prosecutor submits them to interrogation in the presence of their parents and lawyers.

In the first interrogation, A says: "Whoever killed James did bad. Of course, I had nothing to do with it."

In the second interrogation, when the prosecutor shows them the images captured by the security cameras in the mall, A and B admit, separately, that, in truth, that day they had skipped classes and they had been hanging around with

James. "Then we left him right there," affirmed A, "and we went somewhere else. I told B to take the baby back to its mother but he didn't want to."

In the third interrogation, A confesses: "It was B who did everything. I left B with the little boy in front of a church, I was never on that hill."

In the fourth interrogation, A contradicts himself. He admits to having asked a passerby, by now up on the hill, where the nearest police station was located. "B wanted to leave him at the police station, but the baby resisted. He wouldn't stop crying."

In the fifth interrogation, the prosecutor asks A, who has a brother the same age as James, if he would have abandoned his brother in the same condition. "No," he confessed, "... no, because he's my brother. If I really wanted to kill a baby, I would have killed my little brother. Don't you think?"

In the sixth interrogation, A formally accuses B of having killed James "with a steel bar" and of having thrown stones over the little one "so he wouldn't have to see his face."

Deflagration

The story is as follows. We've got Ismael García, no? Ismael García is a backhoe driver. You know what a backhoe is, right? Well ... it's a tractor that digs holes. They had been digging a three-foot-deep trench for months. Just imagine: to unite Caracas with Maracay by a fiber-optic cable! Months lost in the affair, right? They were around Tejerías, more or less. And nobody notices the gas line that joins up with the highway in Tejerías. No? The workers keep "planting" the cable behind him, as they say, and García goes along digging and digging. About then García lets the heavy steel blade drop and he feels it hit metal, right? The guy gets out and he calls the engineer. They lean over the end of the trench and they see something white, like paint chips. Throughout all of this, imagine, they are re-paving the section around Tejerías and only one lane is open. It's seven in the morning and everyone's trying to get into Caracas, right? A long line of cars, right? Waiting to cross that stretch. Things start to get complicated when García begins to smell gas, right? The guy goes running out of there, just imagine, and all the other workers, too. The drivers on the highway see the race and they don't understand any of it, right? This is how García tells it. After that very little is known, right? Well, yes, the explosion, and then the gasoline tank nearby, and whether García was guilty of not having warned the drivers. ... So many factors, right? And of course, after the explosion everyone came; firemen from Maracay, firemen from Caracas, ambulances, the National Guard, the Aragua Police and even a helicopter, right? A helicopter that flew over the fire, which they had to retire because it was fanning the flames. And afterwards the experts, right? The investigations. The following is the hypothesis. Suppose that García cracks a hole in the pipe with the backhoe. Can you imagine the power of a backhoe? Gas starts to escape, right, through the opening. We know that those pipes carry methane. And they tell us they have a smell, right, methane is scented. García runs, of course. The wretch, right? He could have warned the people. But the guy saves his skin and runs like an animal. Slowly a cloud of methane gas forms, and it envelops everything: the backhoe, the cars, the trees, that whole stretch of the highway ... And at least the wind was blowing towards Tejerías, right? If not, just imagine, the cloud would have reached the gas tank and that's it. The methane is expanding, right? Just imagine a gaseous cloud that is gradually diluting and mixing with the air. People think that any little thing can spark methane off, but it's not like that. There has to be a correct proportion, right, that's what the experts say. From five to fourteen parts of methane for every hundred parts of air to produce fire, no? Any little thing could have produced the explosion: a spark plug in one of the cars, a cigarette, some woman's high heel tapping the pavement ... anything. The experts speak of "deflagration": how the cloud begins to burn up at its extremes and gradually burns in towards the center, toward the hole in the tube. Everything that was within the cloud burned: the cars, the gasoline in the cars, the trees, the people ... Just imagine, seventy dead, right?

Carnal Writing

I.

Like syrup around a post, you came and went. There had never been so much spilled flesh, so much recognition after an anticipated straying. In drops that became foolish due to so much weight, each strand of your hair became humiliated. And with the flower of a desired wound we skimmed towards the impenetrable nucleus of the sheet, biting the stems like exhausted athletes, discovering in pain and damage the worm-eaten face of our fastness.

II.

Your belly is under my fingernails. Flesh that I swallow when, nervously, I draw my fingers to my mouth. The yellowish flow is overturned, brief like the dried-out paste that runs over the half-moon of my fingernails. They would say that there's no greater protein than that aged on my fingers, milked with vigor from the black udder of sleeplessness.

III.

Creature with a drop in its nostril, with a tear that flows

218 ⌗ Antonio López-Ortega

down absolved from its eyelid, with trembling and sheets, with a slight gesture to whoever watches it, with a hand suddenly raised to the opposite shoulder, with a sharp winter running the length of its spine. Creature sitting on the bed, searching beyond the window for an appropriate furrow in the snow's pale nudity.

IV.

I go with your body. I advance with your body. Not with my body: with your body. I have left myself behind. I have left myself at home. It's not my flesh exposed to the air; I am not the one arriving. Flesh that passes through the streets, flesh that throbs. I carry an orifice with a throbbing, I carry a swollen vein, I carry precisely the body that erases me.

— for Nela

Bernardo:

First Relations

February 11

The slow construction of a space. The slow construction of a heartbeat. And the distracted father says: "Your fingers will bleed if you put them in this soil." There won't be any new shoots in the depth of the abyss. Only you, stable as a pole, and the thirst that chokes. A bundle of cilantro comes from the mother's hand, any remote impulse comes. Flesh is a lost shore, flesh is this dilated scar. Like a body opened in two, a heart travels without knowing to what grief it owes a debt.

February 19

There isn't any sand under the telephone, there couldn't be any. They have called me, I know, they have called me for the childbirth. A crackling comes to the ear. An open hand without coins comes. I now have no words in my larynx. And what can I say about the light like a heartbeat, like the pulse of nothing. The mother speaks with elbows, with a broken voice, "Open your forehead to the world, my son, whisper to good fortune the nonexistent dictates." From me, not much, two somber holes, the red sclerotic network and an abdomen like a swelled-up bladder.

February 21
The flesh of dreams. The sensation of being numb before the decisive image. The impulse that reaches the point when life doesn't recognize itself. The black and blue body that cries. The father set aside in the deepest muteness. There will never be so much sobbing; never so much umbilical cord. The idea of having touched something of your very own that was escaping you, with my fingertips. The idea of having seen you moaning, in the hollow center of a death that you now carry in your arms.

March 5
You say, washing some red baby socks, that wringing the fabric gets out more dirt than confronting this other chalky abyss in which the muck doesn't detach itself towards any drainpipe's orifice.

March 18
You see the baby grow with the same colic and crying that your mother once calmed. You say a glass medicine dropper would be enough, while deep inside your intuition tells you that the crying continues in the hollow formed by your hands as you wash your face.

Snapshots

Miraflores

On the television screen, behind the seven microphones through which he speaks to the nation, the President. And behind the President, tilted slightly to the left, the painting of an equestrian Bolivar.

El Agua Beach

The precise moment in which the Finlandia vodka girl— a blond mane enveloping a blue metallic body suit—crosses in front of the old man selling dogfish turnovers.

Movie Poster

A woman in search of emotion. The woman says, "I search for emotions." But she can't find them. She tries and can't find them. She brushes her hair furiously before a mirror and she can't find herself. A woman searches for emotion.

The Vision

The movement—always opportune, always calm—of a basketball player—tall, black, robust, shoulders rounded and delineated—who elevates himself in the middle of any scene—a banquet, a conference room, a dining room where you are passing time with that moment's female companion—and scores.

Marina

The slow boats—sailboats, yachts, sleek racing boats—float at the dock as if it were a watercolor. Behind this picture that I see, the mountains gray from drought only return a silhouette that sustains the composition. Only two passengers are missing—a teenager in a bikini and a little blond girl playing—to insure the final brushstroke.

Modern Times

The word *unisex* seen, or glanced, in the hand-painted sign—an ancient brush that barely managed to define the letters—of a barbershop in San Rafael de Mucuchíes, in the state of Mérida.

Protocol

The mayor of Caucagua's wink—now that the official ceremonies celebrating the anniversary of the city are over—as he pulled the hip flask of rum out of a paper bag to toast his colleagues.

Christmas

For seconds we saw the simultaneous backs of three dolphins as they emerged fifty feet from the beach at Cayo Peraza in Chichiriviche. My son Bernardo retained the image and at any moment he evokes the light stream that sprang from their air holes like a rivulet of spit inverted towards the sky.

Ashes

INCENDIE CRIMINEL AUX ÉDITIONS GALLIMARD.
Un incendie criminel a endommagé, dimanche 17 février,
un bureau situé au rez-de-chaussée de l'immeuble des Éditions
Gallimard, rue Sebastien-Bottin à Paris. Les auteurs de
l'attentat ont brisé une vitre et lancé à l'interieur du local
deux cocktails Molotov. Ceux-ci, selon les enquêteurs, auraient
dû mettre le feu à une valise dans laquelle on a découvert
une bonbonne de liquide inflammable et une bouteille de
gaz. Une lettre anonyme a été envoyée à líagence France-
Presse, lundi 18 février, affirmant à propos de cet attentat:
"Ce monde est à détruire, pas à aménager, il ne nous reste
qu'à construire sur ses cendres, les nôtres aussi."